A
Place
To
Go

Edited by Leila Jefferson

My Time Publications

www.mytimepublications.com

Copyright © 2010 Leila Jefferson

ISBN 13: 978-0-9830518-1-7

First Printing 2010

Library Congress Of Control Number: on file

Printed in United States of America

10 9 8 7 6 5 4 3 2 1

A Note From The Publisher

When I first started this book, it was actually going to be a novel that was completely written by me. I started it, but I didn't feel I could give the characters the different depth and versatility I wanted to. I didn't feel I could bring different scenarios to show the many faces of domestic violence. After sitting on it for a while, I finally came to the conclusion that I was going to do an anthology, and that way, other talented writers could put their spin on it and give the diversity I was originally looking for. Big thank you to the ladies that contributed. Envy, Shay, Rukyyah, Nichole, and Keontay, thank you so much for contributing your creativity to my vision.

A Place To Go came from somewhere personal. I had always had the thought of wanting to open a shelter for battered women and their kids, and since many women stay in an abusive relationship because they don't have a place to go, that's where the name came from. I actually had a dream about this place many years ago. Maybe one day I can bring that dream to life.

It's amazing how many women are, or have been, in abusive relationships. We love hard and we love strong. We're told by society we need to be ride or die and we need to stand by our man regardless. That mind frame will let us allow our men take out their frustrations on the world against us. We make excuses and we cover the truth to protect our men. We wear the shades, the long sleeves, and pants. We say we fell, we say we had an accident, and we tell others we are clumsy.

Ladies, if he loves you, he won't hurt you. That's the bottom line. He won't have you feeling embarrassed when you go to work, school, church, or anywhere in public. He won't make you have to nurse your wounds that he inflicted on you. He won't make you think it's your fault because you made him mad. Love should never hurt...

A
Place
To
Go

Table Of Contents

The Intro

The Intro

"Where we going, child? I need to get back to the house and work on this 7 Up cake."

"Just sit back and enjoy the ride, Ms Agnes."

Ms Agnes looked over at Talia and rolled her eyes as she smacked her lips. Talia was one of the stronger ones she had come across over the years. She was so proud of her that she felt like she had birthed her. "Well, when Sammy throwing a fit 'cause he don't have no 7 Up cake after dinner, I'ma point him right to you."

"Ms. Agnes, I know I've said it before, but it's like I can never express enough how much you mean to me and Sammy. If it wasn't for you…"

"Child, hush. You girls always wanna make me tear up. I know you ain't get me all dolled up so I could mess up this painted on face."

Talia smiled. She loved Ms. Agnes more than words could express. Everyone came together to pull the event off, and no one deserved it more than Ms. Agnes. For years, she had been the backbone that many needed. When they pulled up to the building, Ms Agnes wondered what was going on. She looked at the name on the building. *A Place To Go.*

"Child, what's going on here?"

Talia couldn't hide her smile. "You'll find out soon enough."

Talia parked the car and rushed to the passenger side to help Ms. Agnes out the car. Ms. Agnes' stomach was filled with butterflies. She didn't know what was going on, but she knew she was going to cry. Talia walked her to the building, punched in the security code, and they walked through the gate.

When they walked in the clubhouse, Ms. Agnes lost her breath as tears flowed immediately. "What's going on?"

"Ms. Agnes, we all wanted to come together to show how much we appreciate you. You've given every one of us here unconditional love and support. You've given us strength, hope, and pride. You've raised our self esteem, made us feel safe, and helped us be better women and mothers. Ms. Agnes, you always said everyone should have a place to go and everyone deserved to know their self worth. This twenty five apartment complex is dedicated in your honor, and this day is for you." Talia hugged Ms. Agnes tight. She directed her to a seat at the head of a large table. "Sit back and enjoy, Ms. Agnes. We're about to take you back in time." Ms. Agnes was so overwhelmed with tears she couldn't do anything but comply with Talia's wishes. No one had ever seen the feisty old woman give in so easily. Talia walked to the front of the room and grabbed the microphone.

"Ms. Agnes, I know you still are probably wondering what's going on. We all want to say we love you and no matter what, you will always be in all of our hearts." She pressed a button on a remote and started the slideshow on the projection screen. There were several pictures from the last twenty years. "A Place To Go is equipped to house twenty five women, more if they are rooming together, for up to six months to help them get on their feet. We have an array of clothing, toys, and foods from different companies that donated to the cause. We've coupled with different employment agencies and we arranged a fulltime daycare on the premises as well as counseling sessions. You never turned anyone away, and although I know you prefer to look over all your babies in your house, we figured it would be nice to help you help a few more babies." Talia began to tear up. She had to stop speaking for a moment and compose herself.

"Ms. Agnes, I had absolutely no where to go. My husband had beat and battered me for so many years, and I knew I needed to get my kids in a better environment. I had no job, no money, and if it weren't for my kids, I probably would have killed myself to get away from the beatings. I remember the day I was picking my son up from school. I felt like God sent me an angel when we crossed paths. No words needed to be said as you told me I could come with you right then and there, and you would make sure it was OK. I was terrified, but when Sammy looked up at you, held your hand, and told me it was OK, I believed him and I believed you." She stopped another moment and wiped her face with a Kleenex. "You took me, Sammy, and Precious in with nothing but the clothes on our backs, and you've given us so much more. I love you, Ms. Agnes." Talia let out a slight chuckle. "OK, I think I've boo hoo'd enough. I need to let some other people come up and help me out. Coming up is the first speaker, Jewel."

Talia looked to her left and smiled. Ms. Agnes gasped at the name and covered her mouth. She hadn't seen Jewel since she left ten years ago. She felt a sense of relief when she saw her walk up, gave Talia a hug, and took the mic. She looked so strong and in control in her peach pantsuit. She looked over at Ms. Agnes and blew her a kiss, then cleared her throat. "We all know Ms. Agnes is truly an angel on earth. She's touched us all here in some special way, and here's my story."

The Preacher's Son
Leila Jefferson

Lynn elbowed Jewel in her side. "Here he comes, girl," she squealed. They giggled as Charles approached them.

"Hey," he said.

"Hey," Jewel responded.

"So, wanna take a walk?"

Jewel looked over at Lynn, who gave her the biggest smile. "Umm, sure."

They walked around the park where the church picnic was being held. All the girls at church had a crush on Charles. He was tall, had good hair from his mother, and was so sweet. He was always so polite and had great manners.

"I think you're cute. Why are you so quiet?"

"I talk to my friends."

"Can I be your friend?"

Jewel blushed. "Umm, sure."

"Homecoming is coming up at my school. You wanna to go?"

Jewel would have loved to go to a real school dance with him. She went to an all girl's private school and her parents were strict. "That's not really my type of thing."

"You should go, it will be fun."

Jewel held her head down. "I'm not allowed to date."

Charles lifted her head with his finger. "Leave that to me." He kissed her cheek and Jewel gushed. She quickly looked around to see if anyone had noticed, but they were away from the rest of the church folk. "You looked shocked."

"I am."

"Why?"

"What is all of this about?" Jewel wanted to know what was going on. She knew she wasn't the type of girl Charles would go for although she had been crushing on him for as long as she could remember.

"We've been knowing each other since forever. Well, not really know each other. I just want to get to know you. Is that OK?"

"I can't have boyfriends."

Charles smiled. "I already told you, leave that up to me." He walked confidently up to Jewel's parents. "Mr. and Mrs. Wilson, I was wondering if I could take Jewel to the homecoming dance at my school next Friday?"

"A date?" Mrs. Wilson questioned.

"Jewel's not allowed to date boys. She needs to keep her head in the books," Mr. Wilson said.

"I understand, sir. I'm not asking to be her boyfriend, just to be her friend. My father is driving us to the dance and chaperoning as well. He'll also drive us home."

Charles' father was a pastor at the church and his mother was an upstanding citizen. After a quick thought, Mrs. Wilson didn't see any harm with letting Jewel go out with Charles. He was a good boy raised from a good family, and he was a junior pastor at the church, so they figured he wouldn't be much harm.

"Well," she looked over at Jewel, who was smiling ear to ear, "I guess it wouldn't be much harm."

"Thank you, ma'am. I promise I'll have her home early." Charles gave Mrs. Wilson a hug, Mr. Wilson a handshake, and told Jewel he would talk to her later.

Jewel beamed as she skipped over to Lynn. "He's taking me to homecoming."

"Omigod! You're sooo lucky. Everybody's going to be so jealous!" Lynn squealed as she hugged her friend.

Two weeks later, Jewel was getting ready for the dance. She had on a royal blue, spaghetti strapped dress that fell just above her knees. Her mother placed her pearls on her neck and gave her the matching pearl earrings to put on. "Look at my baby. Charles is a nice boy. He'll be a great husband one day."

"Husband? Last week I couldn't even have a boyfriend, mom." Jewel looked at herself in the mirror. She never considered herself pretty, but she felt she was with her hair in the updo and the light makeup her mother applied. She felt grown and sophisticated.

"Have fun, baby."

Just as her mother said that, the doorbell rang. Mr. Wilson opened it and let Charles and his father in. They chit chatted a few moments until Jewel and her mother appeared.

"You look beautiful, Jewel," Charles said as he handed her a corsage.

"Thank you."

"We'll have her home by ten," Charles' father announced.

"Take your time. We know she's in good hands," Mrs. Wilson said.

Charles showed Jewel the perfect evening. It was her first date and she couldn't have asked for anything more. He got her punch, he danced with her, and he acted as if she was the only person in the room. When friends came over to speak, he made sure to introduce Jewel as his girlfriend, and everyone spoke to her as well. Jewel felt as if she was living a fairytale. Although the dance wasn't over until eleven, they left at nine forty five to have Jewel home by ten as promised. Mrs. Wilson was waiting for her, ready to hear all the details of her first date.

"Mom, what happened to your face?" Jewel asked, noticing her cheek looked red and swollen.

"Oh, nothing, honey. How was it?"

They sat down and she told her mother how Charles was a perfect gentleman. Her mother was ecstatic.

******

After the dance, Charles and Jewel were officially dating. He wasn't too keen on the spaghetti straps on Jewel's dress, so she made sure she always wore sleeves. He didn't much like shorts or skirts, he felt it showed too much skin, so Jewel wore pants or long skirts like Charles' mother wore. In a matter of months, she almost looked like a mini Mrs. Martin. Jewel didn't mind because she loved Charles and would do anything for him. And finally, Charles felt like he found the one.

In class, Lynn asked Jewel to go to the mall. She agreed since they hadn't hung out much since she had started dating Charles. She missed her friend. While they were walking around, Jewel's phone rang.

"Where are you?"

"At the mall with Lynn."

"You didn't tell me you were going to the mall."

"She asked while we were in class and we hopped on the bus after school."

"Why didn't you tell me?"

"I knew you had a meeting and figured we'd both be finished around the same time."

"I'll be at your house waiting."

"OK, I'll be there in a little while." Jewel hung up the phone and told Lynn they had to leave.

"We just got here," Lynn whined.

"I know, but he's waiting."

"Jewel, we never hang out anymore. Can't you give one afternoon to your best friend?"

"You're right. Charles will be OK."

Jewel and Lynn finished window shopping, walking the mall, and catching up. Jewel got a text.

Where are you?

Still with Lynn

I said I was waiting

I'll be leaving in a few. Luv you

Hurry

"OK, I gotta go for real this time."

"OK, fine," Lynn said. "We need to do this again. Tell Charles there's enough of you to go around, geesh."

Jewel playfully pushed her friend. "What we need to do is get you a boyfriend."

They got on the bus and laughed more until they arrived to Lynn's stop, then Jewel called Charles to let him know she was almost there. He didn't answer the phone, so Jewel left a message.

Soon as Jewel stepped on the porch, she was greeted by a backhand slap to her face. "When I tell you to do something, you do it immediately."

Jewel held her face in shock. "Did you just hit me?"

Charles grabbed her by her arm, told her to unlock the door, and soon as she did, he drug her to her room. "Were you talking to anyone? Did you give anyone your number? Give me this phone!" He tossed Jewel on her bed and grabbed her phone from her hand. All he saw was calls and texts from him, Lynn, and her mother. The text telling her mother she was going to the mall enraged him. "Next time, you make sure I know where you are before you go anywhere." He threw the phone at Jewel and hit her in her forehead. He let out a sigh and then plopped down on the bed next to Jewel. "I love you so much. I'm scared of losing you." He rubbed her forehead that looked like it was forming a knot. "I'll die if you ever leave me for someone else."

"I love you, Charles. I'd never leave you."

"I'm sorry I hit you. I'll never do it again."

As Jewel was walking Charles to the door, her parents came home. "Charles, my man. How's it going?"

"Good, Mr. Wilson. Jewel told me she wasn't feeling well and I came over to check on her."

"Are you OK, honey?" Mrs. Wilson asked.

"Yea, mom. Just a little bug."

"I'll see you tomorrow after school," Charles said before he left.

"Get some dinner ready," Mr. Wilson said and then disappeared to the room.

"You know, Jewel, you have to learn not to make him mad. Charles is a good boy. Sometimes, it's best to stop running behind those fast tail friends of yours. You're dating a preacher's son. If you're out acting up, then that reflects on him."

Jewel didn't know how her mother could tell Charles was mad, but she didn't question it. "Yes, mother," was all she said.

The next day, Charles came over with roses for Jewel. "I'm sorry," was all he said as he handed her the roses.

At Jewel's graduation party, Charles got down on one knee and asked her to marry him. Of course, Jewel said yes. They had found out two weeks prior that she was pregnant and they had to get married fast before people added things up. Jewel planned to stay a virgin until marriage, but Charles convinced her they would be getting married anyways, so it didn't matter if he got a taste early. After that first time, he wanted it all the time. It was nothing special to Jewel, but he liked it, and she wanted to make him happy. When she couldn't have sex with him, he would get mad at any little thing, and he would push her or grab her while yelling at her. She knew her dad would hit her mother sometimes, but they were still together and mostly happy, so she figured that's what couples did.

They got married two weeks later at their church. By the time Jewel was to start college on a full scholarship, everyone knew she was pregnant and school would have to be put on hold. Charles got a job working with Mr. Wilson at a factory and he hated it. His parents paid the deposit and first three months' rent on an apartment for them, and his father told him as a man, he was going to have to take over things from there.

Jewel had a hard pregnancy that kept her sick. She didn't want to have sex, and Charles ended up going out more, getting drunk with his friends, and sleeping with different women. Since he was the preacher's son, they would go out of town and do their dirt.

Charles came home drunk and made Jewel have sex with him. "You don't know how it feels to be expected to be perfect," he ranted. "They said you were a good girl, but you can't even give me good sex." Charles looked at Jewel like he was disgusted. "Now Tamika, she loved sex. She always gave it to me, and anyone else that wanted it. That slut." Tamika was the girl Charles was dating at his school that his parents didn't approve of. They told him she would bring their family shame. Her nor her family even attended church. Charles grabbed Jewel by her throat. "You sure I'm the only one that's been in this?" Charles let go of her throat and roughly opened her legs. She could smell the beer on his breath as tears streamed down her face.

"Charles, please, you're hurting me," Jewel managed.

"You're fat. You don't even turn me on." Charles turned and walked out the house.

The next day in church, Charles left the youth ministries every so often to check on Jewel and make sure she was OK. He would always kiss her cheek and tell her he loved her. The whole congregation thought they were the greatest looking young couple. They thought Jewel was so lucky to get an up and coming preacher man Charles was sure to become. On the outside, he was a hard working man taking care of his family. On the outside, he was a Godly man that taught the way of Jesus every Sunday to the youth of the church while she helped teach Sunday school to the first and second graders. On the outside, everybody envied them.

On the inside, Charles was a drunk and a cheat. On the inside, he was mean and took his frustrations out on his wife. On the inside, he hated Jewel and the bullshit façade of a life he had to pretend he was living.

* * * * * *

"Get in here and fix me a plate."

Bianca was six weeks old and wearing a young Jewel out. She was tired. The small, one bedroom apartment was cramped and irritated Jewel. Jewel drug her tired body in the kitchen, and warmed up some spaghetti and put some salad on the side of the plate. She grabbed a beer from the fridge and took everything to him.

"What the fuck is this? This isn't my usual beer."

"Money is kinda low so I had to go with a cheaper brand," Jewel whispered.

Charles threw the bottle at her and hit her in the arm. "You're fuckin' useless."

Jewel refused to let the tears fall. She knew it would only make him torture her more. Jewel talked to her mother about it, but she told Jewel that was what all men did, and all she had to do was be a proper church woman and things would be OK. She told her to pray on it and everything would be fine. When Jewel told her mother Charles would slap her and throw her against walls, her mother said she needed to figure out what she was doing to make Charles mad and fix it. Long as he wasn't punching her, things were fine.

Everyone thought they were so perfect, they had started counseling young couples that wanted to get married. They would sit there and act like the doting couple, and told couples how praying and staying in church would keep their marriage strong.

Jewel often wondered why no one truly looked in her eyes and saw the sadness. She wondered where was the counseling for her because she really needed it. There were times they would be on the way to church in the mornings and Charles would curse her out and punch her in the head. While pulling up in the driveway, she would dry her tears, straighten herself, and walk in the church with her head high.

One night, Jewel had just gotten the baby to sleep and she was wore out herself. It was different being a new mother and it zapped all her energy.

"Where's my fuckin' food?" a drunk Charles asked when he walked through the door.

"Babe, you're drunk and you're not even going to eat," Jewel drowsily said.

Rage appeared again and Jewel knew what was to come next. Charles snatched her up from the couch and threw her against the wall. "I don't care if I eat or not. You don't do shit but sit your lazy ass in this house all day. I do all this church shit to pay the fucking bills and you should have me some food ready." He put his hands around her throat. "Do you fuckin' understand me?"

Teary eyed, Jewel responded, "Yes." She tried to walk over to the fridge to find some leftovers for him. As she was thinking she was about to leave his grasp, he slapped her hard enough to split her lip.

"I don't know what I ever saw in your sloppy ass." Charles stormed back out the house, leaving Jewel crying on the floor.

"Where did I go wrong?" she asked herself.

She knew her young, nineteen year old body looked worn and tired. Her golden brown skin didn't have many marks, at least not to the naked eye. If she let go of the turtle necks and long sleeves, the evidence of choking and grabbing would be shown. She was thankful that Charles didn't want others to know how violent his temper could get. He once choked her until she passed out when she was six months pregnant. She was terrified and her mother did nothing to protect her. At first, she thought it was just because he loved her so much because that's what her father did to her mother.

When Bianca was eight months old, Jewel was at the grocery store getting more formula and pampers. She would catch the bus across town. She didn't have enough money for both since Charles spent the money drinking, so she stole a few cans of formula to get Bianca by. She did that for almost a month before she was approached by Ms. Agnes. She had been on her weekly trip shopping for groceries and noticed the frail girl with the small baby bundled in a carrier on her chest. She easily noticed the girl was stealing, but she said nothing. She saw her a few more weeks and once she had seen enough, she finally approached Jewel.

When Ms. Agnes tapped Jewel's arm once she turned the corner from the store, Jewel thought she was security, or even worse, the police. She wanted to run, but she had Bianca strapped to her and didn't want to risk hurting her baby. She felt so stupid for endangering her sweet daughter and risking being exposed and making Charles madder.

She took a deep breath and turned around, only to find Ms. Agnes standing before her. She was even more confused than when she thought she was going to jail and they were going to snatch her baby away from her.

"Listen, chile, I don't mean to give you a fright. I've seen you over the past few weeks and I just want to help," Ms Agnes said in a sweet, loving voice.

Jewel didn't know what to do. The small lady looked to be someone's grandmother, Jewel's grandmother. She was about 5'3 and had beautiful long hair. Her pecan colored skin was flawless and her dark brown eyes had a twinkle Jewel had never seen before. She wore simple black slacks and a white shirt, and something about her gave Jewel a sense of peace she hadn't had in a long time.

"I can't," Jewel softly said and rushed off.

Ms. Agnes let her go, but she knew she would be back. Three weeks later, she saw a timid Jewel enter another store a few blocks away. Again, she witnessed her buy a few cans of formula, and that time, stealing some baby food and diapers. She was pretty crafty, but Ms. Agnes had a sharp eye. After Jewel left the store and turned the corner, Ms. Agnes approached her again.

"Chile, I don't know what's going on in your life, but please, let me help you."

Jewel was visibly shaking and didn't know what do to. "If I leave and he finds me, he'll hurt me," she whispered.

"No one will hurt you. Let me take care of you and the precious one."

Ms. Agnes took Jewel's hand, and again, Jewel felt a sense of peace. Without a second thought, she found herself following Ms. Agnes to the station wagon. "I don't have any money," Jewel finally said.

"Chile, everything's covered. You just worry about finding yourself and being a stronger person for that little angel. What's her name?"

"Bianca."

"What a lovely name. How old is she?"

"Almost nine months." Before she knew it, Jewel broke down crying. "It hasn't always been like this. Charles loved me at one time. I don't know what I did wrong, but he stopped. My mother says I'm not being a good wife, and she said sometimes men hit you because you're the closest one to them. She said I should suck it up and be a woman. I pray every night he'll love me again, but it doesn't work."

Ms. Agnes finally pulled up to her house and parked. She turned and looked at Jewel. "Chile, no one, and I mean no one is another person's punching bag. It isn't right and it's not acceptable." Bianca started to cry. "Come on, let's get little momma in the house and get you two settled."

For the first two weeks, Jewel did nothing but sat in the room and cry. Although home wasn't the best place, it was something she knew, something she was comfortable with. Ms. Agnes was an angel, but she feared Charles would come looking for her and hurt Ms. Agnes or the other girls living there. She wanted to call her mother, but she knew her mother would only convince her to go back home and suffer. She almost even called Lynn, but she felt embarrassed to call her and let her know what was going on.

"Chile, I would never want anyone in my care to be sad. Talk to Ms. Agnes. What do you want?" Ms Agnes hugged Jewel and rocked her like a baby. She knew the first few weeks were hard. Women went through a plethora of emotions and often wanted to sulk and not see a brighter day.

"What am I going to do, Ms. Agnes?"

Ms. Agnes stopped rocking Jewel and made sure they were face to face. "You're going to be strong for yourself, and for this sweet little girl you have. Now, what is it you *want* to do?"

"I thought I was going to go to school and get a business degree. I wasn't sure what I really wanted to do, but I always knew I wanted to work for myself. I feel so trapped. What if Charles finds me? What is the church going to say?"

"Hush now, chile. We can take you down to the community college and get you enrolled. I can watch Bianca while you go to school and work. We'll go to the city about thirty miles north. I figure if your husband was looking for you, I would have heard something by now. Ms. Agnes keeps her ear to the street. And, that church, you don't worry about that. If they are truly God's children, they will understand."

"I can't believe he don't even care that we're gone." That seemed to hurt Jewel more than anything.

"Now you listen here. Don't let no man catch hold of you when you don't even know yourself. Now, the good Lord blessed you with this," she pointed to Jewel's head, "and this," she pointed to Jewel's heart. "You use 'em both and be the best Jewel you can be. Understand me?"

"Yes, Ms. Agnes."

"You can't sit here and wallow in self pity. If you let him hold you, he got you. Now, are you ready to be free?"

A lot of thoughts ran through Jewel's mind. Since she had met Ms. Agnes, she had done nothing but take care of her and Bianca. She took care of Bianca when Jewel didn't have the strength to live. She hadn't forced Jewel to do anything, but she knew it was time for her to come out of her shell and start her life. When she thought about it, she was ready to be free. "Yes, Ms. Agnes, I am," Jewel finally responded with a bright smile.

Ms. Agnes returned her smile. "I knew it was time, chile. Come on, let's get out this room and get some fresh air."

Ms. Agnes introduced Jewel to the two other girls that were in the house when she first got there, and pointed to the room where the newest girl was. She had just come two days ago and she was still in her sulking stage. She gave her a full tour of the house since she didn't get one when she first came. The kitchen was huge. Ms Agnes loved to cook, but the other girls wanted to chip in and cook a meal or two themselves when they could. There was a den with a big screen TV, a dart board, and a pool table. There were five bedrooms and two and a half bathrooms. Two of the bedrooms had two bunk beds and two chest drawers. There was a TV with several DVDs and an array of toys. Two rooms were set up as single bedrooms, Jewel figured they were for new girls to get used to being somewhere different. The final bedroom was a kid's haven. The walls were bright and colorful, and the bedding matched. Disney Chanel was playing on the TV and there were a couple kids on the floor playing games. There was a Nintendo hooked to the TV as well. Jewel could tell Ms. Agnes was mindful of everyone involved.

Ms. Agnes attended church every Sunday and she always invited the girls to go with her. If they weren't comfortable going out, there was Bible study every two weeks, and they weren't required to attend. Ms. Agnes wanted to be low pressure, but she always wanted to offer options. Jewel ended up attending Bible study and then felt comfortable enough to go to church. Within a few months, she was again teaching the children's Sunday school class. She felt the only way she could go on and set her demons free was to confront her husband. Ms. Agnes offered to go, but Jewel felt she needed to go on her own.

Ms. Agnes had a funny feeling about the whole situation so she had Travarus, her unofficial security guard, follow Jewel just in case. It was a good thing she did. Charles was livid the second he saw her. He had already been drinking and the house looked a mess. He roughly snatched Jewel in the house and Travaris knew he heard some glass shattering and muffled screams. He called 911 and tried to wait, but he got out the car and walked to the house. He looked through the window and saw that Charles had Jewel pinned against the wall with a knife to her neck. She had a trickle of blood coming from her lip and her eyes were beginning to swell.

"You're making me look like a fucking fool in front of my parents and the church! Everybody asking where you are and I have no answers! Where the fuck have you been!" he yelled. "Who you giving it to?"

Tears streamed down her face. "No one," she whispered.

"You're lying! Someone made you think you good enough to leave me." He kissed her lips roughly. "Well, if he can have it, I can, too. Besides, you are my wife." He let out an evil laugh as he ripped open her shirt. He began to unbuckle his pants.

"Charles, please," Jewel pleaded.

He punched her and threw her to the ground. "I should kill you. I told everybody you had been cheating and I found out, and your slut ass ran away. And they thought Tamika would bring shame." Charles let out a deranged laugh.

Travarus couldn't wait any longer. He busted through the front door with his gun cocked. "Let her go!" he yelled.

"Kill me 'cause I'm gonna kill her!" Charles said and then stabbed Jewel right before Travarus shot him.

"If that knife had been one inch to the left, I wouldn't be here today. Ms. Agnes has always been my angel."

An eleven year old Bianca came from the back. "Ms. Agnes, you've helped us a lot, we'll always love you." She walked toward Ms. Agnes and gave her a single red rose.

All Cried Out
Rukyyah

Chapter 1
In the Beginning

When I was a teenager, I knew I was beautiful. I had a ton of pictures to prove my confidence, but after years of being with Timothy Walker, he made me feel less than my beautiful self. In the beginning, everything was fun. We loved each other and I felt like we loved each other equally strong. I felt like it was real love because who else would love me so much that he would catch the city bus with me to and from work every day? Tim would even miss days from his job just to make sure I got to my job safely.

Kyra Smith was the name that my father gave me. My father wasn't in my life, but I had a stepfather at home. He loved me like I was his own blood. I loved him so much, more like how a daughter loved her real father. I loved how much my father loved my mother, too. He'd do anything for us. So, growing up with my mother and stepfather did not contribute to why I accepted abuse in my relationship with Tim. Some would like to believe that abuse was a pattern from generation to generation, but I thought they were way off. I never once saw my mother get abused. I never once heard her talk of my real father abusing her. It wasn't until my mother was dead and gone that I found out that not only was my real father a cheater, he was a beater, too.

When I was about fifteen, me, my sister, and my brother moved to Bywater in Annapolis. My mother suffered from Huntington's Disease, so her sickness left us on our own.

I met Tim on the city bus. I was leaving the Annapolis Mall with my best friend, Juanita. I didn't even notice that he was on the bus until I was ready to get off. Juanita and I were having so much fun and laughing about whatever it was that we were talking about, I didn't notice his stare. She looked at him and then at me.

"Best friend, why this nig straight checking you out?" she whispered.

I didn't even let him know we were talking about him. I continued to laugh it up like before. Finally, he came over and sat next to me in an empty seat.

"You are so pretty." He smiled. "What's your name?"

"Kyra." I smiled, showing off my dimples.

"I'm Tim. Can I get your number before you get off the bus?"

"Sure."

Tim was polite, a gentleman, at least that was what I gathered from when I first met him and from our first date. It was summer time when we went downtown Annapolis for a bite to eat. It was evening time, right before it got dark, and it was still warm outside. I watched people feed the birds and his conversation had me hooked on him from the first date. He kisses even made me feel good inside. I was tingling and wanted to know how he'd feel inside of me. As a young girl, I was shy when it came to sex, so I never would have told him how sexually attracted I was to him. Not so soon, anyway. I was sixteen and he was twenty, but he looked eighteen. His butter smooth light brown skin, thick lips, and curly hair were enough to keep the panties wet every time I thought about him.

One of my first jobs was working for a restaurant right outside of Eastport. One night, Tim came to my job and waited for me to close everything down. I made sure I locked the door just in case people didn't read the sign in the window stating that it was closed.

"You so sexy, Kyra. Can I be your man?" He smiled at me while I was caught up in the trance of watching his sexy, thick lips. "Can I have you?"

"Oh, um, yeah." I blushed.

He pulled me closed to him and slid his arms around my waist. His hands dangled over my ass and I guess the roundness made him want to feel it. He did, and then he rubbed it because he noticed there was no panty line.

"You don't have any panties on?" he asked with excitement written all over his face.

"I have on thongs."

"I bet you nasty, ain't you?"

"No."

I wasn't lying because I wasn't experienced enough to be considered nasty. I had a healthy sexual imagination, but I didn't act on the thoughts because growing up in a neighborhood like Bywater, everybody was in your business and everybody knew who was fucking who. I was private about who I shared the goods with so that my rep wouldn't be tarnished.

Tim lifted me onto one of the tables and that shit turned me on. I was a big girl, about a size fourteen, so to have someone pick me up the way that he did make me feel good. He laid me back on the table and lifted my shirt up. He moved my thong to the side as he searched my goodies with his tongue. When I was on the verge of cumming, I damn near jumped off the table because the feeling was foreign to me. He held me down while stiffening his tongue so that I could cum.

"Oh my..." I screamed out while cumming all over his face.

He stood up with his face shining with my juices dripping down his face. He grabbed a napkin and then wiped his face clean. "I knew you would taste good."

I sat there smiling, feeling grown as hell. Later that night, I went home and I felt like a new women. I no longer felt like a teenager dreaming about sexual acts. I was happy to say that I was actually experiencing it. Oh, what a good feeling it was.

"Girl! I didn't know they put their tongue in it," I said real happy into the phone.

I couldn't wait to tell my best friend that I had my goodies licked. She was on the phone cracking up. She enjoyed sharing freaky stories, especially since the both of us were just starting to experiment in the sexual department.

After multiple times of Tim tasting the goodies, he finally got tired of teasing his dick. We had sex at his job for the first time. After that, we were fucking at least three times a week. He would call me all the time and check up on me and make sure I was where I said I was.

"Why that fool always gotta know where you at?" Juanita asked. "Can you chill without having to beep him?"

"Because he loves me."

"Girl, it sounds like he thinks he owns you."

"Well, I am his girl."

"But, you ain't his property. He lucky I ain't answer the phone. I would have hung up on his ass." She laughed.

"Whatever."

It didn't take long before Tim was everywhere I was. He was at every family function I went to and my family loved him. His mother wasn't cool with me, but I didn't give a care one way or another about how she felt. One day when I got home from school, I saw a floral delivery service looking lost, trying to find the house they were delivering to. I was thinking, *Who get flowers delivered in the hood*? The delivery man approached my house and tried to pronounce my name. My eyes widened when I saw the card. Tim had a dozen of roses sent to me and the card had some cute poetry written on it. It was stuff like that, that had my ass falling fast for him. Everybody said that young love didn't last, but I knew that Tim and I would prove them wrong. It was such a good feeling to be loved by him.

Chapter 2
Here Comes the Tears

"Why the fuck you got that shit on with your fucking titties hanging out?" Tim yelled at me one day when he met me at my job.

"My titties aren't hanging out!" I looked over my titties and the cleavage was covered way more than it was when he met me. Before we were a couple, I had titties out for days. He stared at me as if I disgusted him.

"That shit is foul. Don't let me see you wearing shit like that anymore."

"These are my damn clothes and if you want to buy me some more, then you go ahead."

The next day when I got home from work, all of my shit was gone. He threw away all of my shirts that he thought were too low cut. My feelings were so hurt because I didn't have money to shop like that. I was making $7.15 an hour, so I didn't have money for extras. I dropped down to my knees and cried. When he came over that night, he got me a few new things, but it still wasn't the same. It was ugly and it looked like some shit his mother should be wearing.

"You gon' wear this shit from now on." He was trying to sound nice. He walked over to me, started kissing me, and holding me tight. "You know I love you, right?"

"Yes."

After three years of dating, Tim asked me to marry him. My family was against it. They thought I was too young and should wait awhile longer, but I didn't care because I was in love. We had planned to get married the following spring. He got me a cute ring that I felt was a symbol of his love. I couldn't wait to be a family with Tim.

By the time my nineteenth birthday came it was summer, I had my driver's license, and a new car. Tim had stayed over my house the night before. I was excited about my car, but he was acting salty the whole time. He barely touched me.

"So, do you want a big wedding, Tim? You know my family is big."

"Right now, I don't even know if I want to marry you."

"What?" I looked at him with hurt in my eyes.

"You changing, Kyra. I don't know what the fuck wrong with you. You always doing shit with your friends and your family. I bet they telling you, you need to be with a better man, ain't they?"

"What the fuck are you talking about?" Nobody in my family or my friends talked bad about him. "I'm doing the same shit I've always done, and my family was here before you and they will be here after you," I said calmly.

"Why the fuck you yelling at me!" he yelled.

"You are the one yelling, crazy mafucka." I chuckled at me cursing at him.

I walked over to my dresser, and then I bent over to plug in my curling iron. Before I knew it, Tim jumped up out of the bed, grabbed my shirt, and ripped it off of me. He pushed me to the floor and then he threw my torn shirt in my face, causing my hair to be shuffled across my head.

"Say something else. You better not ever talk to me like that again!" He stormed out of my room and left.

I was so happy that my sister or brother wasn't home because I knew they would have killed him. I stayed in my room and I cried myself to sleep.

I didn't even realize that I was late for work. I almost didn't go, but if I didn't work, I didn't get paid. I climbed out of my bed and got ready for work. I kept playing the thoughts over and over in my head. I had my mind made up that I was never going to talk to Tim again. I was ready to kill him. He kept calling my cell phone while at work, and then finally, he showed up at my job.

"Can I talk to you for a second?"

"I'm busy." I didn't even look at him.

"I'm sorry, Kyra. I'm just feeling the tension between us. You got a car, you doing things with your life, and I'm still living with my mother. I know eventually you gonna leave me." Tim broke down and cried.

Watching him cry, I felt like it must have been sincere. *Why else would a man cry in front of his woman unless he really loved her?* I thought. I reached out, gave him a hug, and wiped the tears from his eyes. He pulled me into an embrace and started kissing me with so much passion, I knew he loved me deeply.

It was about three months of Tim treating me like I was his queen. We went out to dinner and movies, and I was feeling that love all over again. I had invested so many years into our relationship and Tim made promises that he would never put his hands on me again.

It was a Monday when I decided to surprise him by going to his job since he always showed up at mine. I was wearing a cute summer dress with no panties, so I planned to surprise him with sex for lunch. I walked in the building and I didn't see him right away. I kept walking until I came across his office. I saw his name, so I tapped on the door twice, but there was no answer. About five minutes of standing outside of his office door, Tim came rushing up on me.

"Kyra, you gotta go."

"What? I just got here." I was confused.

"I know, and you gotta go. They don't like visitors in the office." He was pushing me in the direction of the door.

I thought it was odd because they had a center specifically for visitors. I looked Tim up and down, and I felt like I could kick him in his damn head. I was feeling all sexy in my cute dress and he was pushing me away. I got in my car and I drove back to my house. About an hour later, I got a call from an unknown number on my cell phone.

"Hello," I answered.

"Is this Kyra."

"Yeah."

"I saw you today at Tim's job."

"Who is th..."

"My name is Ashley. I was in Tim's office when you came by. Tim and I have been fucking for six months."

I almost dropped the phone when she said that. My eyes quickly filled with tears, but I didn't let her hear me cry. "And, why are you telling me this?"

Before she could answer, Tim was walking through my door carrying a box of chocolates, a teddy bear, and roses. "Kyra, baby. I'm sorry I had to rush you off, but I ain't want get in trouble on my job." He kissed me and then gave me the gifts.

"I'm on the phone, Tim," I said coldly.

"Kyra, I just wanted to let you know that Tim and I are through. He's a fucked up son of a bitch! He put his hands on me today because I told him that I was tired of being his secret. I was gonna let you know everything when I was at the office, but that motherfucker scratched my face up and choked me out." I heard her crying. "If you stay with him, you're stupid." She hung up the phone.

"So, who the fuck is Ashley?" I threw the roses in Tim's face.

"Who?"

"Don't play me, bitch! You know who the fuck I'm talking about. She just called me and told me every fucking thing." At that point, I was in tears and was shaking.

"She lying, Kyra. Come on baby, you know me better than that." Tim started crying and holding me.

"Take this shit and get the fuck out of my house."

"You don't mean this, Kyra. I love you." He cried so hard that snot was dripping from his nose.

That was the moment I knew that Tim cried at the drop of a dime. At first, I thought it was sweet and it felt good that he shared his emotions with me, but then his crying was more frequent and kind of bitch like.

I picked up my cell phone. "I am calling my brother and my sister to let them know that you are no longer welcomed in my house."

Tim's crying came to a halt. He smacked the phone out of my hand and then he jumped on me. He pulled my hair and then he choked me out. I swear, I must have blacked out because all I remembered was the pain. I tried to focus my eyes, and I heard him telling me how I was never going anywhere. He wasn't going to let me up and leave him.

"You can have any of them lil' mafuckas out there and you think I'm gonna let one of them have you? What the fuck I look like?"

After choking me, he helped me to my room so that my brother and sister wouldn't see me banged up and crying. Every time we fought, he made sure they weren't home. He made sure he didn't leave any marks to make them suspect he was fighting me. That night, I cried myself to sleep and woke up in Tim's arms. I was getting ready for work and I looked down at my engagement ring. At that moment, I knew that I'd never marry him. I took it off and left it on the dresser. In the middle of my shift, Tim showed up at my job.

"Why the fuck you take my ring off? You are my goddamn wife and everybody should know it."

"Get out of my face."

"Put on the fucking ring before I..."

"Before you what? Choke me out in front of everybody in at my job?"

"Wait 'til you get off, this shit ain't finished." He stormed out of my job while putting the ring in his pocket.

That night, I didn't want to go home because I knew he would show up. I asked my close cousin, Pam, to pick me up after she got her son from daycare since she was close to my job. We hung out, and I was too scared to tell her, my friends, or anybody in my family that Tim was fighting me. It was an embarrassment. I thought that they would think it was all my fault and I was provoking him to hit me. I thought that they would think I wasn't keeping him happy, but the harder I tried with Tim, the more he beat me. My cousin and I went out to dinner and she kept staring at me.

"You know, you just don't see like the same Kyra I grew up with."

"Is that a bad thing?" I almost wanted to confess my fears, but I couldn't and I didn't.

"No. You are always in the house if you not at work. You really don't do much with the family anymore."

Truth be told, Tim didn't like me spending time with my family. He thought they would discover his dirty little secrets. He even distanced me from my friends. Being in the house and working at the restaurant, I had gained like fifty pounds. I no longer felt sexy. Tim didn't like me wearing stuff that showed off my figure, so I wore clothes way too big because it was hard to hide tits and ass like the ones I had.

"I've been busy, but we're spending time together now."

"I miss this."

"Me too."

Later that night when I got home, Tim was already in my room waiting for me. "My sister told me that she doesn't think it's a good idea for you to be here all the time."

"What the fuck would she say that? You pay bills in this bitch, I should be able to come and go as I please. What you told her about our little situation?" He raised his voice.

"No, but I should."

"Go ahead and see what I do to you." Then, within the matter of seconds, he turned back into the loving and caring Tim. "Kyra, I missed you. Come here so I can rub your feet."

"No thank you." I was scared to go near him because there was no telling when he'd go off.

"I said come here, girl." He smiled.

He pulled me to him and kissed me while making his way between my legs. He knew that licking the goods always took my mind off of everything else. It did for the moment, but I was getting tired of hiding from my friends and family. I was tired of feeling less than my worth.

Chapter 3
All Black and Blue

"Kyra, I got fired from my job today," Tim told me when he walked into my bedroom.

"How in the hell did that happen?" I sat up and looked at him.

"Well, I was taking off too much time."

"You told me that you had leave."

"I guess I used it all on your bitch ass!"

"How the fuck you use it on me?"

"If I wasn't here with you, making sure you at work and shit. You fucking me up for real!" he yelled.

"I didn't tell you to do all that shit. That was your dumbness. I don't need a babysitter and I sure don't need you at my damn job every day."

"I lost my goddamn job because of you and all the fuck you can say is it's my dumbness?"

Tim jumped on me, pushing me to the floor. My head hit the frame of my bed and I had a big ass knot developing. He pulled me over and twisted my hand behind my back. He put his foot deep into my back and I cried out in pain. That day, Tim left and neither of us knew my sister was still home. She worked 3-11 at the hospital, so I didn't know she was in her room fast asleep. I was in my bed sleeping when she put her hand on my shoulder.

"Kyra, what's wrong?"

I jumped in fear. "Nothing. When did you get home?"

"I wasn't feeling well so I didn't go in. I heard Tim and you arguing. Is everything okay?"

"Yes." I gathered a smiled.

"You know you can come to me and talk to me, Kyra." She looked at me with sadness in her eyes.

"I'm okay." I wondered if she heard him hitting me, but if she did, I figured that she would have killed him.

"Okay, go back to sleep." She covered me up.

I wanted to tell her then, but I didn't know what to say. I was losing my identity every day. I wasn't the same woman I was before him. It was that night that I decided to do something more with my life. I wanted to go to college so that I could make more than the $8 an hour I was making at that time working at the restaurant.

That Monday, I went to a local temp agency and applied for a job. They thought it was a waste of talent working at a restaurant because I could type almost ninety words per minute. The next day, they called me to start my first office job. I was so excited. I was making $10 an hour and I thought that was definitely a good start to getting away from Tim. When I was away from family and Tim, I never wore my ring. I told myself that I'd die before marrying a man that would hit me.

That Tuesday, Tim was still at my house because he didn't have a job anymore. He kept trying to fuck, but I had to go to work. Then, he pushed me on the bed and told me that it was his and he could get it whenever he wanted to. He ripped off my panties and tried with all his force to get between my legs, but I kicked him so hard that he felt to the floor.

"Get the fuck out of my way!" I said above a whisper while getting ready for my first day at work.

When I was finished curling my hair, Tim came into the bathroom and tried to pull up my dress. I tried to push him off of me. He pushed me into the towel rack, causing it to fall to the floor. Then, he pinned me against the wall and bit me on the side of my face.

"You think you better than me 'cause you got a job and a car? You ain't shit, Kyra." He bit down again and I screamed out.

My sister jumped out of her bed and ran down the hallway to see what was going on. It was the first time that he was brave enough to fight me while she was home. She swung open the bathroom door and he ran out with the quickness. He left our house and my sister cried with me and told me that everything would be okay as she rocked me to sleep in her arms. She called the police while I was asleep, and she also called the temp agency and told them that I was taken to the hospital for a minor injury and they were okay with me starting the next day.

My sister woke me out of my sleep. There were two officers downstairs. I was so scared and I wished I was died. *I rather be dead than to be a statistic*, I thought. The female officer came to my room and told me it would be okay. She took pictures of the bite marks on face, and the old and new bruises on my body. I felt invaded. I wanted to cry all over. That night, Tim tried to get in my house, but my sister wasn't having it. At that time, my brother had moved out, so he had no idea what was going on.

"You will never see my sister again, and if you touch her again, I will bust your fucking head open, do you understand!" I heard my sister yelling, which woke me from my sleep.

When I went downstairs, Tim was gone and I felt empty. After that fight, he did anger management and about six months later, we were back happy again. Even when he got mad, he would try to control it. It was almost our wedding date and I didn't go through with it. I found out I was pregnant and Tim was trying his hardest to be there for me and the baby. He finally got another job making more money and he enjoyed it. For a little while, there were no more fights.

One day after work, I went to local HBC and applied. I'd always wanted to go to college, but I didn't think I could afford it. I got financial aid and I was happy about that. Since I was pregnant, I receive section 8 so Tim and I moved in together. He didn't want me to go to college and he would go off every time he thought about it. One night, Tim had my car and was gone for a long time. He claimed he was playing basketball with his friends, but I checked the miles in my car and he had lied about where he went. The following night, he went to play ball again, so I called my sister to use her car. I followed Tim and he ended up at an apartment in Glen Burnie.

"What time your game over?" I had called his cell phone.

"In a little bit, baby." He pretended to be out of breath. "I'll see you soon, love you."

I went back home and took every one of all his shoes and threw them in the dumpster. I left him one of each shoe so that he could have a memory of each of them. I wanted him to know that he shouldn't fuck with me. He was a fan of go-go music, so I threw his collection away, too. When he walked in the door, I told him what I did. He felt down to his knees and started crying.

"That's for you lying because I followed you to that bitch's house. I suggest you go back there." I rolled my eyes and stormed into my room.

That night, he slept out in the living room, and I was wishing he would take his ass back to his mother's house. After all of that bull shit, I still was rolling tight with him.

I have to go to college to get away from him, I thought.

"Look, I ain't feeling you going to college. What the fuck they gon' teach you as smart as you are?"

"I don't care what I'll learn, but I'm going."

"Well, if you go, you can kiss me goodbye because I told you, you ain't fucking going."

The first semester, Tim drove me to classes in my car. He bitched and complained all the time. One night when I was waiting for him, a male classmate waited with me. I was nervous because I already knew I was gonna get my ass whooped when I got home. When Tim pulled up, he got out of the car, pulled me by my hair, and pushed me into my car. I was so embarrassed that he would wild out on me in front of my classmate. Later that night, he took my textbook and swung it full force into my face. I swore my nose was broken.

"You a slut for talking to that nigga. What, you want to fuck him! Well, guess what? You pregnant with my baby. Ain't nobody gon' want you. Who gon' want a bitch with a baby? Ain't nobody checking for pregnant bitches anyway, so you might as well suck it up and marry me."

Was that shit supposed to make me feel better? I wondered.

Every night that I shared with Tim in our home, I cried myself to sleep. I didn't know what I'd do without him because I was having a baby. He was right, not only was I pregnant, but I felt ugly so I knew everybody else thought I was ugly, too. I would go to work and to school. I hadn't talked to my family in months and I missed my sister so much. She was like my best friend. My cousin was about five minutes away from me, and I didn't see her anymore, either.

Then, I got a fucked up wake up call. I got an eviction notice. *What the fuck?* I thought. *I am giving Tim money to pay the bills. This has to be a mistake.* I showed Tim the notice and it didn't come as a surprise to him.

"Kyra, I got fired again."

"What the hell does that have to do with us being evicted?"

"The rent money, I had to use it for something. I had to replace all my fucking shoes, and how the fuck you think we got all that food in the refrigerator and gas in the car?"

"What the fuck good will food do us in that damn refrigerator if we have no place to live?" I cried.

We had a month to get out of the apartment, so we stayed up until the last night. I didn't want to bother my family because I was embarrassed to let them know how bad off we were. We didn't have much stuff in the apartment, so most of my stuff stayed in my car. His mother had an extra room, so I stayed there. I went to work and school as usual. That night when Tim picked me up, some random man held the door open for me, being polite since I was pregnant.

"Thank you." I smiled.

"You're welcome."

Tim got out of the car with the quickness. "That's my fiancée. She's carrying my baby, bitch!" he cursed at the man.

The man approached him and said, "I suggest you take that bullshit somewhere else, ain't nobody worried about you."

The man pushed past Tim and that set him off. He took a swing at him and missed. The man pushed Tim on the hood of my car and smashed his head into it. Tim looked like he was about to cry. I had never been more embarrassed because he was getting his ass kicked in front of my college. It was the night I knew that he only had stretch over women. That night, he kept looking at me funny.

"I'm not feeling staying here, I'm just gonna call my sister."

"No the fuck you not! You staying with me!" he yelled.

He got up in my face and twisted my arm behind my back. He pushed me down to the floor and I was scared that my weight and his would smash the baby.

"Get off of me!" I cried out.

He pushed me into the door knob and banged my head against the wall. "Stop this shit before you hurt the baby," he told me.

I knew he lost his damn mind. He went to the couch and laid down, and I stared at him so hard, like I wanted to kill him. I jumped on him and scratched his face up. I choked him so hard that his eyes rolled back and he started foaming at the mouth. He pushed me off of him and then he punched me in my mouth, which made me stop fighting him.

"I said stop this shit. You fucking pregnant!" he yelled.

That night, I didn't know where to go, but I remembered at my college they were handing out flyers about domestic violence and had a few local numbers if you needed help. I kept the flyer in my car because I always knew I needed help, but didn't know who I could trust. I sat in my car rubbing my stomach while telling my baby that we would be okay. After talking to a counselor on the phone, the friendly woman told me she knew someone that could help. She gave me Ms. Agnes' number and I called. When I spoke with her, she told me she would meet me at a neutral spot, a local diner. I took down the address and I went there. I sat in my car for a minute because I felt like I couldn't share what I'd been going through. I looked through the window of the diner and saw a woman with an aura of peace around her. Almost instantly, I wasn't scared or nervous. I looked in the rearview mirror and saw my busted lip, and I knew I needed help. Not being able to face my family, I got out of my car and took baby steps to the front door. I was greeted by a smiling face, and Ms. Agnes became my angel that night.

Chapter 3
A New Beginning

Ms. Agnes fed, bathed, and clothed woman and children from all races, all ages, and she didn't judge not one of us. At first, I'd go to work, go to school, and then go to my room to cry myself to sleep. Ms. Agnes always made sure that I ate because I was pregnant. I had lost my appetite, so she would fix me a bowl of soup and feed it to me. After I would eat, I would cry a river on her shoulder.

Every week, someone new would stand up in our meetings and tell the group what brought them in Ms. Agnes' care. I couldn't tell my family that I was there, so I knew damn well I wasn't going to tell some strangers why I was there. Then, the more I listened to their stories, I felt like I could share with them. It took me three weeks to finally speak up and share. Ms. Agnes told me that she was so proud of me.

After sharing my story, I felt it was time to contact my family and let them know I was okay. It was a month after being there and Ms. Agnes contacted my sister. My sister and my cousin came and they were so sad that I didn't reach out to them. They were grateful to Ms. Agnes for protecting me and giving me courage to take my life back. My sister was happy to have me back home, but I knew I couldn't stay long with the baby on the way.

By the time my daughter was born, Tim was locked up for domestic abuse. I pawned my engagement ring and with the money, I put down a security deposit to get an apartment far away from Tim, but near family and loved ones. After losing most of my baby weight, I went out and got myself a sexy black dress. It was low cut in the front and showed off my round ass. When I tried the dress on, I knew that Tim would totally disapprove of it. That was what made me love it.

I went to the mall and got my makeup done, and then I did a photo shoot in my sexy dress. I was beautiful again. I no longer hid bruises and I no longer felt worthless. I had a healthy baby girl that I absolutely adored, and she loved me as well. My family had been a big support because Tim often contacted me trying to get his family back, and if it wasn't for their love and caring ways, I would have slipped back into such a loveless relationship. After leaving Ms. Agnes and getting back on my feet, I knew that all of my tears were all cried out.

§§§§§§

Rukyyah is the founder of Erotic Ink Publishing as well as the author of the much anticipated novels *Hood Vixen the Female Hustla*, *Cold as Ice*, *Princess 1 & 2*, and *Satisfied*. Her debut novel, *There's No Turning Back*, solidified her spot as an author on the rise and dazzled fans all across the nation. Rukyyah is a contributor to *Naughty & Definitely Not Nice*, *A Place to Go*, *That's the Way Love Goes*, and *Tasty Temptations*. She's a native of Annapolis, Maryland. Rukyyah is a graduate of Sojourner-Douglas College and The University of Maryland.

Home Is Where The Hart Is?
Envy

Tamika Hart paced the floor, desperately hoping she'd done everything to suit her husband's demanding expectations. She knew if something wasn't to his liking, she'd have hell to pay once he entered their six thousand square foot home. She made her way over to the wet bar and poured herself a shot of Patron. Soft music filtrated through the house as she wondered what he'd nitpick about when he walked through the door.

For what seemed like the hundredth time that evening, she went back into the kitchen and made sure everything was turned down low. She wanted to make sure everything was simmering to stay warm. Rowan Hart liked everything to be hot when he came home. She remembered the time when she let his cabbage get a little too cold. He threw his plate in her face and demanded for her to cook everything over. At ten o'clock that night.

Like the dutiful wife that she'd been for the past several years, she did as she was told. They didn't eat until midnight that night, but he didn't seem to care, as long as he ate. The jingling of the keys broke her reverie. She turned her attention to the door and ran over to greet him.

"Hey, baby. How was your day?" she asked him.

He was a retired professional football player, and he coached the sport he loved. Whenever he walked through the door, he wore the same grim expression, but that didn't stop her from trying to lift his spirits.

"Tired," he mumbled, throwing his keys on the table that sat next to the front door. He said, "Where the hell is my dinner?"

"Oh, baby, everything's ready. I am about to fix your plate. Would you like something to drink? Cognac? Seven and seven?"

She began walking over to the wet bar when she felt an unbearable pain in the back of her head. She staggered a bit, tried her best not to fall, but the heaviness of the impact made her knees wobbly, weak as jelly, and her head was spinning. She was in no shape to stand, so she hobbled over to the couch and took a seat.

Enraged, Rowan stood over her fuming. His chest was heaving up and down and his eyes had turned bloodshot red. His fist came down fast and hard, and she screamed from the intense pain his hand inflicted upon her. She held her hands up, trying to block his hits, but he was too fast and too strong for her. His fist came down hard three more times as Tamika's jaw felt like it was about to cave in. After he grew tired of hitting her, he picked her up by the neck with both hands. She was dangling in the air; her feet weren't touching the plush white carpet and her orbs were as big as quarters. Rowan beat her on a daily basis, but there was something different about that ass whooping. She felt as if she were about to die. As she tried to claw his hands off her neck his grip became tighter. She struggled for her next breath, and he wore a sinister smile. He seemed as if he wanted to watch her take her last breath.

Finally, as if he'd gained some kind of sense, he dropped her. She fell to the floor, coughing and gasping for air. She took a few deep breaths, trying to catch her bearings and get herself together.

"Get your ass up and fix my plate," he said before stepping over her. The tears streamed down her golden cheeks and she tried to pull herself up. Her bones were weak and she ached all over. She grabbed the side of the couch and stood to her feet, hunched over she made her way to the kitchen and fixed her husband a plate.

She placed his plate on the table and poured him glass of lemonade. She then made herself a plate and within a few minutes, he walked into the kitchen and sat down.

"What the hell is this?" he asked, looking at his plate.

"It's a new dish I thought you'd like," she said timidly.

"What's today?" he asked her tersely.

"Look, I know it's pot roast day, but I thought you'd like this and…" He spit in her face, cutting her off. She picked up the napkin and wiped the remnants of his nasty remains off her skin. Everything was so routine, so scheduled for them, and she figured she'd try something new. "I-I'm sorry," Tamika whispered.

"I don't know why you continuously make me mad. Make me do things you know I don't want to do."

He stood up from his seat and Tamika nervously put her fork down, preparing herself for what was about to happen. He pulled her out of her chair as she kicked and screamed, pleaded and begged for him to stop. He kicked her repeatedly in the stomach as she tried to ball up into fetal position. Her stomach felt as if it was about to rip apart.

"Bitch, from now on you stick with the schedule and cook what I tell you to cook. I will let you slide tonight. I'm going out to eat. You eat that Thai shit you cooked."

He left the house as she stood from the floor for the second time that day. Bones bruised and spirits low, she retreated to her bedroom and climbed in her king sized bed. As she laid, she thought about her life and how it had spiraled completely out of control. She'd endured many beatings from him, she was growing weary, and didn't know how much longer she'd be able to take his constant and cruel punishments. Maybe it was God's way of punishing her. After all, she didn't love him when they first married. Dollar signs were the only thing she was interested in when he proposed to her. Already an established quarterback with the Dallas Cowboys, he came with several hefty endorsement deals in tow.

Tamika was poor, dirt poor, and sometimes she didn't know where her next meal would come from. She lived from a homeless shelter to crashing on friends' couches. But, the one thing she did possess that was like a meal ticket was her looks. Men were attracted to her light colored skin, long, bronze locks, and her emerald green eyes. Her shape made many men do a double take, and usually she received gifts and money from them. That's how she got by. She didn't have any skills, just a typical college girl majoring in Broadcasting and living hundreds of miles from home, so she had to do what she had to do in order to survive.

When she met Rowan Hart, she wasn't smitten by him. She didn't find him attractive at all, but her friends thought of her as the lucky one for snagging a rich man. In the hype of it all, she was turned on by the materialistic things he got for her. When they first started dating he was nice, but there was always a dark side. He was extremely jealous and didn't like her to be around other men.

Tamika was in her last year of college when she was forced to drop out. She'd gotten pregnant by him and three months later, she suffered a miscarriage. At first she was a little upset, but years of living with him let her know she didn't want children by him. And honestly, the only reason she'd stuck around was because she wouldn't be able to efficiently take care of herself alone. Rowan had the money. Rowan had the power. Rowan had the respect. Rowan had everything she needed. And, he had her just where he wanted her, in the palm of his hand.

Tamika tossed and turned until Mr. Sandman finally reared his head at around two a.m. Of course, Rowan wasn't home, but at that point she didn't care. With him gone, she got the solace she so desperately needed. When she woke up the next morning, she busied herself with daily chores. Rowan was too cheap to hire help, saying that since she didn't work she could keep the house clean, and boy, did he like it clean. Once a week, she had to clean the chandeliers and windows, and he left her with a cleaning list.

The ringing phone gave her a reason to take a little break. At the sound of her mother's voice, a smile pierced her thin lips. She wanted to talk to her mother and confide in her, but the older lady loved Rowan. She was always calling and bragging about the exquisite gifts he purchased for her. That particular day was no different.

"Oh, baby, Rowan just got me a full mink coat," she gushed. "I am going to be the sharpest woman at church on Sunday. Watch how Sister Hazel and Deacon Porter's wife hate."

Her mama kept bragging on and on about her son-in-law while inside Tamika was heated. Rowan had got in good with her mother just to patronize her she thought. She didn't know how she'd break the news to her mother, but they had to talk. The conversation they needed to have was long overdue.

"Mama, let's do lunch today. Meet me at Donaldson's at one."

Her mama agreed to meet her and Tamika quickly sprinted to her closet to see what she'd wear. Her mother was not only observant, but she scrutinized everything Tamika wore. Ever since she was a child, nothing was ever good enough for her mother. The only time she'd made her happy in adulthood was when she snagged a professional athlete. And, today she would have to tell her mother she was thinking about leaving Rowan. In her heart, she knew her mother wouldn't accept the news, but Tamika had to do what she felt was best for her.

She could've beat her own ass for not securing a better future for herself, but it was too late to think of putting aside money now. She didn't know if she could tolerate Rowan for much longer.

Finally, she decided on a conservative blue Donna Karen suit. After she showered, she dressed and applied makeup to her nearly flawless skin. Her skin was once as smooth as a baby's bottom, but years of Rowan's abuse had left inevitable scaring. Some added to her beauty. Tamika's beauty was so exquisite, it would take a lot to make her look bad. She winced from the pain of pinning her hair up. Upon close observation, one could tell how Rowan had pulled plugs of her dark and gorgeous locks out her head. After pinning her long hair up into a neat bun, she slipped her small feet in a pair of Christian Louboutin pumps. Once fully dressed, she smiled at her reflection and promised the woman in the mirror that she'd always take care of her. Tears slipped down her face, but she quickly wiped them away with a manicured hand. Time was slipping away so she grabbed her oversized purse and left the house.

Tamika sipped on lemon water while waiting for her mother, who was almost twenty minutes late. "Mrs. Hart, are you ready to order yet?" the waiter asked while refilling her empty cup for the third time.

She shot the young waiter a tight smile and declined. "My mama should be here in a few minutes," she said, trying to sound hopeful.

"Very well, ma'am. I will be back in a few minutes to check on you," he quipped.

Just as she was about to open her menu, her mama strolled in as if she didn't have a care in the world. For a fifty year old woman, Judi James looked exceptionally well. She'd maintained her size six figure after bearing three children, and her hair was still the same cinnamon color in which it was when she was born. Her skin was still smooth and wrinkle-free. And, her mocha colored skin held no signs of blemishes or aging. Judi was dressed to impress in a peach colored pantsuit and a pair of matching pumps.

"Hey, darling," she quipped. Judi leaned over and kissed Tamika on each cheek. "I am sorry, baby, I lost track of time. I've been shopping at Bloomingdale's with Helen." The waiter came back to the table as soon as Judi took a seat and asked for their orders. To drink, she had a cup of iced tea. "What are you having?" Judi asked, studying her menu.

"Uh, I think I am having the T-Bone steak and potato."

Her mama frowned at her and asked, "Don't you think that's a little too fattening for you? I mean, you miscarried last year and still haven't lost the last twenty pounds to get back to your normal size."

Tamika sucked her teeth, ready to tell her mother off, but the waiter came back to the table. Her mother ordered her favorite, pasta shrimp bake and Tamika, against her mother's wishes, ordered a steak and potato.

"It's your figure," she said once the waiter walked off.

"You're right, and if I want to be as big as a damn house, then that's my business," she said sternly.

Her voice had risen several octaves and the patrons nearby were staring at their table, curious as to see what all the commotion was about.

"Chile, hush, you don't have to get an attitude. I was just trying to help you out."

"Mama, I don't need your help."

"Tamika, what did you want to tell me? You know we can't talk long without arguing, so maybe you should just tell me what you wanted so I can go home."

"That's the problem, mama, you have never showed me the proper attention, and every time I get mad about something you want to run. I called you hear to talk to you. I have something very important to talk to you about."

Tamika really didn't know how to tell her mother what she was feeling. She didn't quite know how to put her emotions in words, but she figured she'd try as best she could and hope her mother would listen to her. She took a few deep breaths, sipped on her water, and said, "I am thinking about leaving Rowan."

"What?!" her mother bellowed.

That time, it was her mother's turn to get loud and everyone in the restaurant stared at them. For the first time in a long time, Tamika had her mother's undivided attention. Her eyes were as big as quarters, perhaps she seen all the extravagant things he did for her flash before her eyes. Maybe Tamika had inherited her money hungry ways from her mother, but that was the old Tamika. Rowan's money didn't excite her anymore. Wouldn't allow her to deal with his infidelity and abusive ways.

"Chile, tell me I was just hearing things because I know you didn't just tell me you were leaving Rowan. He's the best thing that's ever happened to you. What will you do with your life if you leave him? You have no skills," she said nonchalantly.

Tamika could have choked on her piece of bread. Tears welled her eyes as her mother words sunk in her head. How could she put her down like that...again? She took a deep breath, trying to calm herself. The woman sitting across from her was still her mother, so she had to treat her as such.

"Mama, I don't know what I am going to do. But I am thinking about going back to school to finish my degree."

"At your age?" she scoffed.

Damn, another insult, Tamika thought.

Her cold emerald stare held her mother's light brown eyes hostage for a few moments. She wouldn't let her mother upset her. She wouldn't run out the restaurant in tears with her tail tucked between her legs. She'd stand up to her mother, let her know she was in control of her own life and remind her that she was an adult.

"Mama, what is that supposed to mean?" she replied hotly. "I am just turning thirty, how is that too damn old?"

She gasped while Tamika rolled her eyes. Her mother had always been so damn dramatic.

"Why I never?! Don't you ever curse at me!"

Their food arrived, but Judi didn't eat. She gathered her things and left the restaurant, leaving her daughter behind in tears.

Tamika felt like a prisoner in her own home. Day after day, she endured physical and emotional abuse from her husband. Rowan acted as if he didn't even love her anymore. He hadn't touched her in weeks, and she knew it was because he was busy occupying another woman's bed. His infidelity didn't even bother her as much as his abuse did, but unfortunately, she didn't have a choice in which abuse he showed on what particular day. Rowan was a total chameleon. One day he would be fine, and then the next snap out.

She took a few deep breaths while looking at him sleep. He looked so peaceful. She wanted to wake his ass up with scolding hot water. She wanted to stab his ass in the chest with a butcher's knife, but she couldn't see herself going to jail for the rest of her life. His life wasn't more important than hers. She stood over him, watching his chest rise, and then fall. His mouth was slightly open and then, then her attention turned to his ringing mobile. It was a distinctive ring tone in which she'd never heard before.

Who could be calling him at three in the morning?

Slowly, she walked over to the dresser and grabbed his phone. Looking over her shoulder, she made sure he was still asleep. Then, she went into the bathroom and sat down on the toilet. His phone was locked and she didn't have his four digit password. Every number she could think of was the wrong one. His birthday didn't work. His last four of his social security number was wrong. His mother's birthday wasn't the right code.

Damn, he can't be this damn smart, Tamika thought as she played with the phone some more.

Her birthday wasn't the right password. She chuckled because she already knew he wouldn't have anything dealing with her as his secret code. He didn't love her that much. She then put in her mother's birthday and the phone instantly unlocked.

What kind of freak nasty shit is this? she wondered. Out of all the numbers in the world, his password had been her mother's birthday!

She looked through his text messages as her eyes began to water. She always had a feeling he was cheating, but seeing it was something totally different. The evidence was right in front of her face.

I had a good time tonight, can't wait to see you again.

She would've dropped the phone if a burning sensation across her face hadn't have broke her reverie. "What the fuck are you doing with my phone?" he barked.

Tamika got some strength from within to stand up to him. "Who is Monica?" she asked squarely.

"What makes you think I owe you an explanation?" he shot back. She turned on her heels to leave the room and he grabbed her slender arm. "What the fuck do you think you're doing?" he asked.

"I am leaving you!"

He laughed. His laugh broke the silence and filled the huge room. It was a laugh mixed with boisterous contempt and evilness. She pushed past him and pulled out her Louis Vuitton traveling bag and began to pack.

"How in the hell are you going to take care of yourself?" he questioned.

She knew he was right. She had no means to fully support herself financially, but she wouldn't give him the satisfaction of knowing he had her right where he wanted her. She was trapped in his web and at the moment didn't know what she was going to do, but she kept packing.

Once she was finished packing her clothes, she made her way to the door, which Rowan blocked. She could in no way compete with his two hundred and thirty pound frame. He easily outweighed her by at least a hundred pounds. His shoulders were as wide as the doorway and she tried pushing past the brick wall.

"Rowan, please move. Why do you want me here so badly? You're fucking with at least three other women. Move them in here."

He grabbed her arms, his grip tightening by the second. He wouldn't release her and she felt like her arms were about to burst under the magnificent pressure. She tried wiggling out of his reach, but nothing worked. He stared down at her intently. Their gaze met. She didn't look away. Wanted to read his dark eyes. Wanted to know why he'd turned so cold. He pushed her with all his might and she fell back, hitting her head on the iron bed railing and everything around her went black.

Tamika awoke to an almost unbearable throbbing in her head. The darkness of the night frightened her. She knew she wasn't home because she kept her night light on by her bed. Looking down at her body, she noticed she had on a hospital gown. She then took in her surroundings. Immediately, she knew she was in the hospital, but for what?

Tamika pressed the help button and in less than five seconds, a young and pretty brown skinned nurse appeared. She was short, probably around five feet three inches tall, and she wore her short hair in a pixie cut. She was small, maybe ninety pounds soaking wet.

"Is there something I can do for you, Mrs. Hart?" she asked nicely.

"Where, where am I?" she stuttered. Tamika's voice was groggy and hardly recognizable.

"You took a nasty fall yesterday and have a mild concussion. Your doctor should be here first thing in the morning to release you."

Where's my family?" she asked.

"Your husband and mother left a while ago. They'll be back in the morning to take you home."

Tamika closed her eyes as the prior evening's events cluttered her mind. She remembered why she was there. Rowan had pushed her down and made her hit her head. She reached up and felt the huge lump at her temple. Squeezing her eyes shut, she hoped to find a place to go. She didn't have many friends she wouldn't burden the few she had by asking to provide for her a place to stay. And, staying with Judi was out of the question. So many thoughts filled her brain. She worried about things that were out of her control and as she closed her eyes she prayed to God for answers. She'd never been much of a spiritual person, but the only person she could call and depend on was God, so she leaned on Him for help.

Sleep didn't find her that night. She stayed up all night, plotting and planning her escape from Rowan. First thing she planned to do was enroll in college and complete her degree. Then, she'd figure her next step out. Tamika didn't sleep, but surprisingly, she felt better. A smile graced her lips as the sun rolled from behind the clouds and smiled on the universe. She felt light and weightless, and at around eight a.m. the doctor walked through the door holding his clipboard. He'd written her two prescriptions, one for pain and the other for swelling.

"Thankfully you didn't hit your head as hard as you could have. That could have been a fatal hit. You take care of yourself," he said. "The nurse will be in, in a minute with the discharge papers."

She closed her eyes and said a silent prayer as she got out of bed. Her body hurt. From her head to her toes, she was throbbing. It took great effort getting to the bathroom to shower. The only clothes she had were the ones from the previous night and they had blood on them, but she had no other choice. Quickly, she dressed and as she stepped out of the bathroom, the nurse was there patiently waiting for her to sign the proper documentation.

Rowan and her mother walked in, and she threw both of them an evil eye. He came over and gave her a peck on the cheek.

"You ready to go?" he asked.

Incredulously, he acted as if he didn't have a care in the world. She couldn't look at him, could hardly stand the sound of his voice. She didn't want to be in the same room with him, but she couldn't move without thinking. She had to have a plan and thankfully, she'd conjured up one. Rowan and Judi laughed and talked the whole ride home while Tamika sat in the backseat, sulking and feeling like a stepchild. They didn't include her in any of the topics of conversation, and she couldn't help but to feel unwanted and totally out of place. She wanted to cry, but she didn't want to let them see her shed tears over them.

"I am staying over to cook dinner for Rowan," Judi announced.

Tamika didn't say anything, she just retreated to her room, popped two pain pills, and went to sleep. She didn't wake up until the next morning, and her mother and Rowan were nowhere to be found.

Tamika couldn't hold back the tears anymore. In the comfort and solace of her own bedroom, she cried. Her mother treated Rowan more like a child than she treated her. They'd never had a close relationship, but Tamika wanted them to mend their relationship. She wanted to know why her mother had been so cold all these years. Picking up the phone, she dialed her mother's number. She answered on the first ring.

"Mama."

"What do you want, Tamika?"

"I don't want anything. I just wanted to see how you were doing."

"I'm fine."

Judi's answers were short and curt, and Tamika could feel the uncomfortable silence every time her mother stopped talking.

"Mama, I want to see you. We need to talk."

"About?"

Sighing, she slowly stood from the bed and paced the floor. The pain had subsided and she could walk straight, but the pain in her heart remained. "Mama, I want to talk face-to-face with you. It's important. Can you come over today?"

"No, I am going out with your sister today."

"I'm sure Tamera can wait, mama," Tamika whined.

An impatient sigh escaped Judi's lips and Tamika could feel the agitation through the phone lines, but that didn't deter her from trying to convince her mother to come over.

"Please?" Tamika begged.

Finally, she gave in. "Okay, Tamika, but I can only be there for thirty minutes," she replied.

Tamika smiled. She had hope that they wouldn't bicker like the last time they were together. "Thirty minutes is perfect. Thank you."

With that, she ended the call. Everything had to be perfect when her mother came. She needed an explanation and only Judi could answer all the unanswered questions she'd kept bottled up over the years.

The doorbell chimed just as Tamika was taking the tea off the burner. She pulled the pastries from the oven and placed them on the island. She sprinted to the door and looked out the window. Strangely, no one was there. Slowly, she opened the door and stepped out on the porch when she felt something thick and heavy under her feet. Looking down, she saw a manila folder. She scooped it up and went back inside the kitchen. The folder was from the Child Support Offices and it was addressed to Rowan Hart.

Child Support! she thought.

Her hands trembled and her breathing quickened as she ripped open the folder. Rowan was being sued by a woman named Monique Green for child support. He was being ordered to take a paternity test for a baby boy named Rowan Ellis Hart, Jr. Tamika dropped the papers and they scattered across the floor. It was bad enough that he'd gotten someone else pregnant, but the bitch had the audacity to name the baby after her husband.

Oh, hell no! She dialed Rowan's mobile and he pressed the ignore button. She knew he did because her call went straight to voicemail. Hanging up, she walked back into the kitchen. She was numb from the pain of finding out about Rowan's child. She'd wanted a baby so badly and every time she got pregnant, he'd stress her out so bad she'd lose the baby.

Her mother arrived fifteen minutes later, and she was still in a trance and really couldn't deal with trying to talk to her mother. So much was on her mind and she knew she couldn't tell her mother because she always sided with Rowan.

"Mama, why have you always been so hard on me?" she asked, pushing aside her problems.

"Tamika, I always expected more out of you than your sisters. You were the smartest, the prettiest, the level-headed one, and when you dropped out of college, I was so upset."

"Mama, you've been treating me differently since I was a child. Why?"

"You reminded me so much of your dad," she said.

Finally, the truth was coming out. Tamika covered her mouth as her mother explained everything to her. Her father's betrayal, the real reason behind his death, and she couldn't believe it. Tamika's father was black and Asian, and Tamika had inherited his striking looks. From his wavy, long hair to his green eyes, even his features. She was so much like him.

Fredrick James was a lady's man. He loved running the streets and he was a doctor. A gynecologist. When his mother found out about his affairs with a few patients she was heartbroken. He wanted to divorce her for Elizabeth Franklin. But, when her husband found out about his wife's betrayal, he couldn't handle the deceit. He walked in on Liz and Fred having sex and blew their brains out.

Tears flowed as Judi recanted the story. It was like she was reliving that painful experience all over. Fredrick was her everything, her first love. The only man she'd been with. Her children's father, but he didn't care about leaving her with three girls. He didn't care about her needs and wants. He was just being a man, selfish and inconsiderate. Tamika shook her head and cried as her mother talked. She was a little too young to remember what had happened and her mother had shielded them from all her father's demons, but the whispers had been all around town. Everyone knew her father wasn't any good and all the teasing forced Judi to pack up her and the girls and move. She couldn't take the stares. She couldn't take the smirking. Tamika always thought that they'd moved to be closer to her grandmother.

"Mama, I...am...so...sorry," Tamika said between sobs.

They hugged as they cried in each other's arms. Judi because of the recently revealed skeletons, and Tamika because of the papers she'd picked up from her doorsteps a few hours earlier.

Tamika was waiting on Rowan when he arrived home. She was sitting in the living room, holding the papers in her hand. He walked in and sniffed the air. He didn't smell any dinner cooking and he was ready to get to the bottom of it. Tamika needed another ass whooping to solidify who was really in charge around there. He turned the corner and became hot as hell when he saw Tamika sipping from a flute of wine, yapping away on the phone.

"What the fuck is going on and where is my dinner?" he demanded.

"Monique, I am going to call you back." He was taken aback by the mention of his lover's name. She threw the papers at him. "I want answers! What the fuck is this?" she asked.

He looked down at the child support papers. That dumb bitch had actually gone through with it. She'd told him she was going to do it, but he hadn't believed her. He thought as long as he was giving her that good lovin', everything was going to be alright.

"What are you doing opening my goddamn mail!"

"That's the only time I know anything around here," she quipped, standing from the couch. He slapped her across the face and she fell back on the couch. The strike was so powerful she landed on her stomach. She wiped the blood from her mouth as she stood and ran into the kitchen. Rowan was close on her trail, but she ran like her life depended on it. She pulled out the butcher's knife and turned toward him. He was so close the knife touched his chest.

"Take another step toward me and I will kill you."

"Oh, so you're a killer now?" he said.

"Only if I have to be." She gave him a look like, 'try me,' and the smoldering intensity in her gaze let him know she wasn't playing.

He turned on his heel and said, "Get your shit and get the fuck out my house."

Tamika had eighty three dollars to her name and didn't know what she was going to do. As she sat on a bench nearby, she looked through the newspaper, trying to find the nearest shelter. No one would believe that she was the wife of the famous Rowan Hart. At least not at that moment, she looked like orphan Annie, throwing on anything to get away from Rowan in his erratic state. At the griping of her stomach, she stood up and went into the store. She needed a sandwich or something. She pulled out her oversized Chanel sunglasses from her purse and put them on her face, trying to hide the many bruises. She pulled her hair over her shoulders and walked in the store. As she walked through the deli part of the store, she noticed a woman staring at her from the corner of her eye. The older woman smiled at her as she pushed her basket filled with groceries down another aisle.

Home Is Where The Hart Is? by Envy

Damn, I ain't with that carpet munching shit, she thought as she walked through the produce section. She placed a few things in her basket before making her way to the register. The older woman with the gray hair came right up behind her. Tamika shot a tight smile her way and she smiled back. The older woman reminded her of her grandmother. She was short and motherly looking. Her gray hair was pulled up into a bun and the flower dress she wore was comfortable looking. She looked like the average grandmother. Tamika looked away, careful not let anyone see her face. She shifted her weight from one expensive stiletto to the other as she waited for the cashier to announce her total. Readjusting her frames, Tamika looked in the distant at the children playing outside of the store. So carefree and joyous, she remembered those days all too well.

"Your total is $22.55," the cashier said, pulling her from her lucid thoughts.

She swiped her card. Waited…and waited. The card was declined. "That can't be right. Let me try this again," she said. Tamika looked behind her and apologized to the older lady.

"Take your time, baby," she said sweetly.

She swiped it again. Declined again. "There must be some kind of mistake. Let me call the bank," she said, stepping to the side.

She was about to pull out her phone when the older woman stopped her. "Just add her stuff to my total," she said to the cashier.

Tamika went to protest, but the older lady stopped her. When everything was paid for, Tamika walked out with the older woman and helped her put the grocery in the car; that was the least she could do.

"Thank you so much, baby," she said graciously when everything was securely in her backseat.

"No, thank you, Ms."

"Agnes," the woman answered.

"Okay, thank you so much, Ms. Agnes."

"No problem, and if you ever need anything, please, don't hesitate to ask. I am only a phone call away."

Ms. Agnes handed Tamika a card with her name and address on it. She ran a haven for women who've been abused.

Tamika looked down at the card and wanted to say something, but she couldn't bring herself to ask for help. Again, her foolish pride wouldn't allow her to say anything. She thanked her, and then hugged her. As Ms. Agnes drove away, Tamika went over to the pay phone and sifted through her purse for change. She called her mother's house and Judi answered.

"Mama, I need to come home for a minute," she said.

"I am sorry, Tamika, but you can't come here."

Tamika could have choked on her tongue. What did her mother mean? She thought that they'd broken the tension between them the other day when they'd had their heart to heart talk, but now her mother was acting brand new again.

"Mama, why?" she asked.

She was confused and didn't quite understand her mother's reasoning.

"Tamika, Rowan helps me with the bills and stuff, and I don't want him to cut me off," she said truthfully.

"So, you choose him over me?" Tamika asked.

It was a huge blow and she couldn't believe the words that were coming from her mother's mouth. She could have reached through the phone and slapped her mother for being so stupid, but she decided to just let it go. Let it all go. She didn't need anybody but God and Ms. Agnes. She didn't wait for her mother to say another word, just slammed the phone down and walked away.

For the next few days, Tamika spent all her time on the street. She didn't have anywhere to go and the harsh winter months were making her sick. As she sat on the bench in the park, she pulled her coat tighter as she trembled from the harsh winds. She couldn't take it anymore.

Standing from the bench, she began pacing back and forth, trying to get warm, and then an idea popped in hear head. She pulled out Ms. Agnes' number and sauntered to the nearest pay phone.

"Hello." Ms. Agnes' voice poured through the phone like rich honey. Just hearing her made her warm in the inside. She took a few deep breaths and told her she needed help. "Where are you?" she asked, sounding alarmed.

Tamika told her where she was and in a few minutes she pulled up to scoop her up. Tamika got into the car and graciously thanked her.

"Don't worry about it, this is what I do. This is what I love. I've devoted my life helping young women and children. Maybe that's why I've never had children, but God has been good to me."

The short drive to her house was a pleasant one. Tamika studied the two story home in front of her and smiled. From the outside it looked very homey, but there was still a little hesitation on her part. She was scared to trust anyone, but she couldn't go back to the streets. Her bank account was nothing to brag about and she didn't even have enough money to get a hotel room. Taking a few deep breaths, she peered out her window. Her mind went someplace else.

"What's wrong?"

The concern was etched in Ms. Agnes' voice. She didn't want the older lady to feel bad, but she was skeptical about the situation. She didn't really know what to expect. "I don't know...about...this," she said, her voice trailing off.

"Baby, I don't want you living on the streets. If you don't stay with me, where will you go?"

She had a point, and Tamika took her words into consideration and decided to stay with Ms. Agnes. She climbed out and followed Ms. Agnes inside the house. She looked around. Everything appeared to be immaculate. The wooden floors in the living room sparkled.

"Would you like a grand tour?"

Tamika obliged. She wanted to know what she was getting herself into. She followed closely behind Ms. Agnes as she walked through the living room and turned to the left into the kitchen. The appliances were stainless steel and the walls were painted a bright yellow in color. The lightness illuminated through the small kitchen. She led her up the stairs, which led to five bedrooms and two bathrooms. Her bedroom was the first one to be put on display. The red and black décor was breathtaking. The room was tidy and nice, and she had her own personal bathroom. Her bed was full sized and on the wall rested a 32' flat screen television. The plush carpeting was butter cream in color. Her bathroom was peach and teal and she had a walk in shower and a Jacuzzi tub.

Tamika followed her to the first room. This room was for the battered mothers with children. The room held two bunk beds and a corner filled with toys for various age groups.

"Tamika, this is Connie Brown and her daughter, Tiara."

After the introductions were made, Tamika shook the younger woman's hand. Connie appeared to be in her mid to late twenties and she was pleasant on the eyes. Short, around five feet tall, she was slim and wore her hair in a short Fantasia inspired crop. Her copper colored skin looked like it had been blessed by the sun and her facial features were pretty. Her large, expressive eyes held a sadness, though, and right about her mouth was a huge scar. She looked like she'd been cut from the corner of her mouth up to right under her eye. But, thankfully the scar didn't take away from her outer beauty. The little girl stood behind her mother and seemed to be very evasive. She didn't say much, but she was a very pretty little chubby girl with really big ponytails. She was probably around eight or nine.

The woman seemed to be pretty nice and Tamika learned she was taking up psychology and currently enrolled in Clark Atlanta University. There was more for her to see, so although Connie's conversation was pleasant and enlightening, she followed Ms. Agnes to where she'd be staying. The room in which she'd be occupying was vacant at the moment and she silently thanked her Heavenly Father because she'd never been a fan of staying with a lot of females, not even in her college years. The room held two bunk beds and she placed the little things she had on the bottom bunk. The room décor was blue and the comforter matched the walls perfectly. The last room was for women with babies. The room held two bunk beds and a couple bassinets.

"This is Angela Miller and her son, Bryan, and this is Leticia Powell and her three month old daughter, Sabrina."

Tamika shook both ladies hands and played with their beautiful, bouncing babies. That meeting didn't last long either because Ms. Agnes wanted to talk to Tamika, so the two retreated to the living room. Tamika made herself comfortable while Ms. Agnes went to fix them some tea.

While she was gone, Tamika looked around, taking in the living room. So clean, the floors could be eaten off of and the room was so spacious. The fireplace was lit and that was the only light bouncing off the walls. But, still in the darkness, Tamika could tell that Ms. Agnes took great care in cleaning her home.

Ms. Agnes returned with a tray. It held two cups and a saucer of chocolate chip cookies, Tamika's favorite. The plate barely touched the table before Tamika started choking down cookies. She was starved and felt like she hadn't eaten in weeks, rather than days. Ms. Agnes watched her eat, went and got her more cookies, and then watched her some more. Letting her eat until she was full, Ms. Agnes just smiled pleasantly as she offered to fix her something to eat.

"No, this is fine. Please, don't go through too much trouble for me," she said.

"Tamika, it's not any trouble at all."

"What made you want to help us?" Tamika said.

It was the first time she'd ever admitted to being homeless and helpless. The feeling wasn't good, but she was ready for her breakthrough and the only way she could turn her situation around was to not be in denial. She took a deep breath and listened attentively to what Ms. Agnes was about to say.

"I've always loved to help. Always wanted to help women in particular fulfill their dreams in life, so opening up my doors for women has been fulfilling and a blessing all at the same time."

"But, what made you know that this was what you wanted to do?" Tamika asked, putting more emphasis on her question.

Ms. Agnes' expression became strained. Troubled a bit. She put down tea cup and stared off in a distance. She looked like she was trying to gather her words. Finally, she said, "I just felt it was my calling in life."

Ms. Agnes asked Tamika about her life, the life she was running from, the life she so desperately needed to escape from. Tamika wasn't coy at all, she told Ms. Agnes everything.

Ms. Agnes listened attentively as the young woman talked about her upbringing, her life with Rowan, and how she felt she brought the situation on herself. She reasoned that since she was a gold digger when she first met Rowan, karma had come and bit her in the ass.

"Baby, you didn't do anything wrong. You were young and naïve, and just wanted stability in life. There are a lot of girls like you. Your situation ain't no different and don't you go blaming yourself, you hear? There's no reason why a man should be hitting a woman," Ms. Agnes concluded.

Ms. Agnes was so easy to talk to and Tamika opened up to the older woman, taking her advice and helping her make plans for the tedious future. Life without Rowan would be hard, but not impossible. The first step was to go and sign up for school and find a job. Even though she lived with Ms. Agnes, she had to be able to support herself. The hour was growing late and it was too late to do anything, but Ms. Agnes promised to take her out to look for jobs the following morning. Ms. Agnes showed so much concern over Tamika's well being and it brought tears to the younger woman's eyes. Tamika's own mother didn't care enough about her to take her in, but thankfully, Ms. Agnes stepped up to the plate. Tamika and Ms. Agnes hugged while Tamika thanked the older mother figure again.

Six months later….

Life had changed drastically for Tamika and she would forever be grateful to Ms. Agnes for taking her in. It was a very special day, as she would be graduating from Clark Atlanta with her bachelor's degree in journalism. There were already a few job offers on the table, but she would be content with just keeping her job as assistant manager at Macy's for now. Tamika was doing good for herself. She'd divorced Rowan and taken half of his fortune. With the money, she built a brand new home and invested some money in Ms. Agnes' business. Ms. Agnes was in the crowd as her name was called. The convention center erupted in applause as Tamika walked up in her Jimmy Choo stilettos to obtain her degree. She was overcome with happiness as she thought of all the things she had to endure to get to this point in her life.

That day was her breakthrough. Finally, she'd accomplished her life goals and her future was looking bright. As she made her way to her seat, she found Ms. Agnes, who mouthed the words, "I am proud of you and I love you."

Of course, her mother wasn't there. Probably somewhere nursing a cancer stricken Rowan, but with Ms. Agnes being there, she didn't need anyone else, not even her mother.

The next one hundred and seventy graduates were called over the next half hour and the graduation ended after writer, Karen Miller, gave a moving speech. Tamika admired the older woman and aspired to be just like her. She'd made a lot of power moves in the literary game. Tamika ran up to Ms. Agnes and took her in a warm embrace. She appreciated everything Ms. Agnes had done for her, and Tamika would forever be grateful.

"Baby, you are so welcome. Helping you wasn't a problem. I am always here for you and if you ever need anything, you know I am only a call away."

Tamika and Ms. Agnes went out to eat to celebrate Tamika's graduation.

"Baby, what are your plans?"

Tamika took a bite of her mashed potatoes and thought for a while. Although the future was a lot brighter, she still didn't have a clue as to what she'd be doing with her degree. She was just grateful to finally have one.

"Well, you will figure it out. You've figured everything else out."

Ms. Agnes looked at Tamika with pride, never had she met someone so determined, so set on making the best out of her life. She had no worries that she'd make it and tears glistened her eyes.

Tamika looked up from her plate and sighed. "Ms. Agnes please don't start crying again," she begged.

"I just can't help it, you've made me so proud," she admitted, dabbing her eyes with a piece of tissue.

Tamika smiled at the older woman; she thanked her Heavenly Father for her everyday because without her, there was no telling where Tamika would be. She needed the motivation she'd given her.

"Ms. Agnes, I have a surprise for you," she chimed.

"Me?" Ms. Agnes asked before saying, "Baby, I don't need anything. Just seeing you accomplish your goals is enough for me," she admitted. The waiter scurried back over and placed another helping of mashed potatoes in front of her. "Ms. Agnes, you're not having anything else?" Tamika asked.

"No, I am trying to control this cholesterol, honey. Everybody can't have a sleek size eight figure like you."

"I worked hard to look like this, trust, I am only eating what I want today. Tomorrow, I will be back on my strict diet. I wish I was naturally petite and could eat whatever I want, but as I get…" Tamika stopped in mid sentence as Rowan and her mother walked in the restaurant. They were holding hands and being really friendly with one another. "Ain't this a bitch?" Tamika said.

She had meant to keep that in her head, but the words accidentally slipped out. Ms. Agnes' gaze followed Tamika's and fell on the couple. She wondered what was going on and asked Tamika.

"That's my mother and ex husband," she replied.

Tamika was so upset, her vision became blurry. She wanted to go over and punch Rowan in the face and curse her mother out for not being there for her, for picking money over her own daughter, but she had to keep her poise and worry not about her mother or Rowan's sorry ass. God was already taking care of him, she'd heard through mutual friends that he'd been diagnosed with bone cancer. She hadn't seen him since the finalization of their divorce, and he'd lost at least fifty pounds in three months. Tamika's mother appeared to be having a good time, though. She was mingling with the enemy, being friends with the man who'd beaten her daughter time and time again. Tears welled up in Tamika's eyes, but she refused to let them fall. She refused to let her mother and Rowan get the best of her.

"Honey, are you ready to go?" Ms. Agnes asked gently.

Tamika watched the chemistry between her mother and ex-husband as they were seated a few tables down. The couple seemed to be in their own world, and Tamika wanted to go over and give them both a piece of her mind, but she had to remain calm. Causing a scene in a popular restaurant wouldn't be reputable to her career. Even though she loathed the scene before her, she had to contain her bearings and leave with Ms. Agnes. She hadn't talked to her mother in a while and she decided to keep her distance. Besides, she didn't need her, Ms. Agnes filled the void that had been empty for so long.

"Yes, I am ready to go."

Tamika grabbed her Louis Vuitton bag and made her way to the door. Her mind was in another world as she followed Ms. Agnes to the front door. Out of nowhere, someone bumped into her and she felt warm gravy on the front of her blouse. An expletive escaped her lips as she jumped back and tried unsuccessfully to wipe the food off her Susan Fergammion dress. Both women were looking down.

"Oh, dear I am so sorry," the stranger said.

Tamika knew that voice from anywhere. It belonged to a heartless bitch. Their gaze met. Tamika's held malice. Her mother's, shock and confusion.

"Hello, mommy dearest," Tamika snarled.

Judi stood back and studied her daughter. Couldn't believe how good she looked. "Tamika?"

She laughed. "What did you think I was going to do, fall apart because of Rowan? Did you honestly think I'd be pining over him six months later? You see, mama, I've moved on, made things happen on my own. You don't know what I've accomplished because you didn't want me in your life. You threw me away the day Rowan threw us away, and for that I will never forgive you. I just want to tell you that I've graduated and have a few job offers on the table. I am an assistant manager at one of your favorite stores, Macy's, and I am doing alright for myself, no thanks to you."

"Tamika, you didn't understand. Don't understand now, but..." Her voice broke from unshed tears.

She was about to cry, and that time, Tamika didn't feel sorry for her. She couldn't show empathy for the woman who didn't love her. She looked at her mother in disgust and began to walk away.

"Wait!" her mother yelled.

Slowly, Tamika turned around and faced the woman who'd birthed her. Judi hurried over to her and looked in her eyes. She wanted Tamika to see the hurt in her eyes, the pain she'd harbored for years. Judi's words were stuck in her throat. She wanted badly to make amends with her daughter, but didn't know how to. The healing process would be long and slow. That was even if she allowed her back in her life. Judi reached out to Tamika and she stepped out of her reach. Tamika had all guards up when it came to her mother. She'd disappointed her, her whole life. Tamika didn't want that time to end like so many times before.

"Mama, I don't need you now. When I did, you were nowhere to be found. Chose Rowan's sorry ass over me, your daughter, your own flesh and blood, but that's okay, I won't cry over spilled milk, but you will be taken care of. You will definitely reap what you sow," Tamika spat, looking at her mother as she walked away.

"Tamika! Tamika! Baby, please!" her mother yelled after her, but that time, Tamika kept walking. She had a beautiful future ahead of her and her mother wasn't in it.

§§§§§

Envy is an ambitious writer who dreamed of sharing her vision and talents through literature. *Sexual Eruption* was Envy's first published collection of erotic stories. She is a contributor to *A Place to Go* and *Naughty & Definitely Not Nice*. She is currently working on several novels. Envy is working on finishing her degree in Elementary Education. She lives in Holly Springs, Mississippi with daughter.

Someone To Live For
Nichole

Dear God, if You could just let me get through this night, I promise I won't do anything to trigger his anger so that he won't beat on me anymore. That was the beginning of my nightly prayers. It was not one day of my life with Carlos that I was free of being abused. Whether it was mentally, physically, emotionally, sexually, or verbally, I knew I was going to be abused. I was terribly frightened by his abusive ways and his strength. Carlos was thirty six and stood 6'3, muscles toned his dark skinned sexy body. His short hair with waves was always shaped up. He carried anger most of the time, and I guess it was his job. He worked at an accountant firm and it was always stressful, so I understood why he would get upset sometimes.

At times, he could be sweet, but sometimes he took it way too far. I didn't know why he felt the need to take his anger out on me all the time. I was thirty four, just a lil' ole skinny light skinned, girl that stood 5'4 that wore my hair in a ponytail. There was nothing impressive about me. I don't work because he didn't want me to. I didn't hang out with my friends and family because he didn't want me to. I wanted to start college just to get away from him, but he didn't want me to. I had no way of getting around because Carlos didn't want me to have my own vehicle. I didn't do anything that he didn't want me to.

Anything that would set Carlos off, I would suffer the consequences. I knew one day he would hurt me, maybe even kill me. I tried to escape so many times, but I was afraid of what Carlos would do to me. Whatever he did to me was not a pretty sight to see, literally. He always left me with bumps and bruises. So, I knew if anytime I decided to escape, that I had to keep going without looking back. And, that's what I did, I kept going.

It was early Sunday morning, October 3, 2009. I remember that day so well. We had a terrible rain storm the night before, which made it a little foggy that morning. I knew that Carlos would sleep in that morning because he had a few drinks the night before. We stayed in as usual, and I made dinner that he decided that he didn't like that night, and he got angry about that.

"Mya." That was short for Amiyah, which was what he called me. Carlos closed the door and locked it. He turned toward me as I was sitting on the couch that was facing the door and watching TV.

"Yes, baby?"

"What you cook?"

"Hamburger and French fries."

"I don't want no hamburger and French fries. If I wanted that, I could have stopped by McDonald's to get it. I just got home from work and I am starving. I want something else," Carlos yelled as he unbuttoned his suit and threw the jacket on the couch, hitting me in my face.

"I already made your plate for you. It's in the microwave."

Carlos walked past the couch I was sitting on straight into the kitchen, his face filled with anger. He reached for the microwave handle on the door, pushed the button to open it, and pulled out his plate. He then purposely dropped the plate on the floor.

"I'm not eating this," he said with a calm voice, looking at me with his evil eyes.

I began getting nervous because I know it was about to turn into something ugly. I sat on the couch with my mouth sealed. At times, it would be best just to keep quiet and do as he said to avoid the physical abuse, but either way, whether I was quiet or not, no matter how big or small, I was still abused when things didn't go Carlos' way.

"Clean this mess up, now!" Carlos yelled.

I sat on the couch. My eyes flooded with tears that gently ran down my cheeks onto the palms of my hands as I held them in my face, covering my eyes and hanging my head low toward the floor. I guess I sat one minute too long. Just as I was slowly rising up from the couch, I looked up and felt a smack on the side of my face.

"Carlos, stop it!" I screamed, holding the side of my face where he slapped me.

I looked at him and within seconds, he grabbed my arms with both hands and squeezed me as tight as he could. I began crying more, the pain was unbearable. Before I could reach up to protect my face, he punched me in the mouth and then pushed me over the couch. I laid there in a fetal position with my head buried in the couch pillows to protect my face from being used as a punching bag. Carlos continued to yell and scream, telling me that I was no good and no one would want me because I wasn't worth anything to a man.

Every day, Carlos would attack me with his verbal abuse. Once you heard over and over again that you were no good and no man would ever want you, then you start believing it was the truth. I loved Carlos and I thought he was a good person, he just had some anger issues that could be worked out. I didn't think he meant all the negative things he said about me. I never thought I'd be in a relationship like that. If he would get another job that was less stressful, then maybe he would be happier and not take things out on me.

As I laid on the couch in my fetal position, I noticed blood on my shirt and felt something dripping from my lip. I wiped my mouth and realized my lip was bleeding. Carlos eventually stopped screaming and went to our bedroom in the back of the house. I stayed on the couch and cried myself to sleep.

The brightness of the next morning awakened me. I laid on the couch to get some more rest, and then I heard footsteps walking down the hallway. I slowly sat up on the couch, looking around and preparing myself to be ready in case Carlos decided to attack me again. Already dressed for work, he bent down toward me and gave me a hug and kiss as if nothing happened the night before. I was used to that behavior, after almost all the fights he would award me with gifts or affection, but none of that mattered anymore. I was finally fed up.

"Look at your lip." He hugged me and begged me to forgive him for what he had done again. "I will never do this to you again," Carlos promised. "You need to go to the Urgent Care, just tell them you fell down the stairs or something." He wanted me to lie to protect him. I was tired of protecting him. I had been protecting Carlos for the last three years that we had been together. "Go to the bathroom, take a shower, and put some makeup on so you can drive my car to drop me off at work while you go to the doctor," he suggested.

Getting up from the couch, I slowly stood to my feet. I took one step at a time because my body was so sore and bruised from Carlos beating on me. I managed to make it back to the bathroom. I undressed myself and it took all the strength I had left in me to look at myself in the mirror. My eyes were puffy from crying most of the night. I stared at myself with no self esteem. I cried some more as I saw my busted lip and how bruised up I was.

This is it, I convinced myself. *I have a chance to escape from Carlos.* I thought about the consequences if he caught up with me and found me. I didn't know where I was going to go. I took a shower and then dried off. I wrapped my towel around me and went into the bedroom. I got dressed and put on some makeup to cover the marks on my face. I put on something that would cover up most of my bruises. I pulled my hair back in my usual ponytail and walked out into the living room where Carlos was waiting for me.

"Drop me off at work, then go to Urgent Care down the road from my job, and come right back home. Don't try to pull no stunt, Mya, because you will regret it," he threatened. "Get your emotions together, you're okay."

I was a good actress, I was used to the scene, pretending like nothing was wrong. We walked out the door and got into the car. The sun was shining, but it was a little chilly. I dropped Carlos off at his job.

"See you this afternoon, Mya."

I said okay and watched him as he walked into the building. I sat in the car thinking. Knowing Carlos, he would walk down to the Urgent Care to see if the car was there since it was walking distance of his job. I decided to go see a doctor. I pulled up to the Urgent Care in Somerset Village Shopping Center in Charles

Town, WV, the same town where Carlos and I shared an apartment together on Main Street. I walk up to the receptionist.

"How may I help you?" she asked. I let it be known to her that I needed to see a doctor for my bruises and pain. "A doctor can see you in fifteen minutes."

Thank goodness it wasn't crowded as usual. The receptionist gathered my information and asked if I have insurance. I informed her that I did not. She then motioned me to have a seat until I was called back. I sat for around ten minutes watching TV. I was still thinking about how to plan my escape from my relationship with Carlos. I couldn't go home to my parents because I didn't want them to know about the abuse. Nor, did I have any friends to call on. I had no clue of how I was to escape, but I was praying that an idea came to mind.

"Amiyah Mitchell," a nurse called. She appeared to be in her late twenties, brown skinned, and short hair. She was very tall. She took my weight, blood pressure, and temperature. She led me into the room where the doctor would exam me. She introduced herself as Gina Brothers. "What brings you here today, Amiyah?" the nurse questioned.

I told her I was in pain and that I fell down some stairs as I was in a hurry leaving out my apartment on my way to work. She asked me to get undressed, left a gown on the reclining doctor's chair in the room, and walked out.

"I will be back in a few minutes. I just want to take a look at your bruises."

I began getting undressed, put on the gown, and within minutes nurse Brothers walked back into the room. She asked me to stand. As I stood up, she walked slowly around me with her clipboard and took notes of the bruises. She placed her clipboard on the table next to a computer and asked me to hold out my arms because she noticed bruises on them.

"I usually don't get all into patients' business. However, I can see that these bruises on your arms did not come from you falling down steps. I can see finger prints on your arm," she mentioned.

I avoided looking at her in her face, but again, I played my role and said, "Oh, nothing is wrong." I was in denial.

"Have a seat." The nurse said. "What's going on here?"

I told her I was okay and that it was nothing. To get her off my back and not to go all into what happened, I went on to tell her that I got into a fight with my boyfriend, but it was both of our faults and that everything is okay.

"I have been around women that have been abused. My Aunt Agnes has been helping women for a long time in these types of situations. She helps them get over the hump in order to start a new life. She has a five bedroom home in Martinsburg, WV. It's a house for women that have been abused. She welcomes single women and women with kids or pregnant as well. Here, take this card, it has her address and phone number on it."

I thanked the nurse with a sigh of relief and thanked God for answering my prayer.

"Give her a call, she will answer any time of the day or night," she said with concern. "I can walk you out to the front desk now and you can pay for your doctor's visit. It's possible if the doctor sees you and realizes the truth, he could make a report," nurse Brothers warned.

I let her know that I would leave the office to avoid any reports being taken and I promised her that I would call her Aunt Agnes. She then explained she would notify the doctor that I left. She opened the door as she told me everything would get better. I paid my fee at the front desk and walked out.

I got back into the car and sat for a few seconds. *I'm going back home*, I thought to myself. *I can't do this. I can't make it on my own.* I said a little prayer and sat for a couple more seconds. Holding the card in my hand, I looked around to make sure Carlos wasn't in sight. I made up my mind to go to the closest store that had a pay phone outside and decided to call Ms. Agnes. I grabbed some change out of Carlos' ash tray, hurried to the phone, and dialed the number. Nervous and trying to hold back the tears, I began speaking after a woman answered the phone.

"Hello, Ms. Agnes speaking," I heard a strong voice speak.

I started to stutter. "Um, um... hello, my name is Amiyah Mitchell and I was given your number from your niece, Nurse Gina Brothers."

"Say no more, young lady, come right on down and Ms. Agnes will take good care of you. I own a nice sized house with five bedrooms," she stated.

I didn't wait any longer. I was familiar with the area since it was the next town over in Martinsburg, WV. I hurried off the phone with her and drove to the address located on Foxcroft Avenue. It took just about fifteen minutes to reach the house. I parked a few houses down and slowly walked toward her house. I walked up the steps to the front door and rang the doorbell. Opening the door was a petite lady who stood at 5'3 and was approximately one hundred and thirty pounds. She looked to be in her late sixties and had long salt and pepper hair. She invited me into the sitting area where she asked me to tell her about myself.

"Have a seat," Ms. Agnes offered. I sat down on the couch and glanced around. She had some pictures of other women and kids. From what I saw so far, the home seem very clean. "Tell me about yourself."

I began to tell Ms. Agnes about my situation with Carlos and all the abuse he had done to me. I shed some tears as I did every time I told the story. I continued to explain to her how I basically escaped from him and ran there after I dropped him off at work. I told her I had Carlos' car. Ms. Agnes immediately called a family member to pick up the car and drop it back off at my apartment complex.

"What time does Carlos get off?" she asked. I told her that he got off in a few hours. She went on to say how it would be best to get the car back to my apartment complex because if Carlos called the car stolen, then they would find the car there and possibly find me. I agreed to give her my home address, and she arranged to have Carlos' car back in a half hour. "As I mentioned to you earlier, this is a five bedroom. You can sleep in the room that's for single women with no kids." I nodded my head in an agreement with her. "I've been helping women to regain their self esteem, teach them to love themselves, and help prepare them to live on the outside world and do for themselves. I have my own private room, but you are always welcome to knock on my door anytime."

She really made me feel comfortable and I was so glad I made the decision to come to this home. Ms. Agnes went on to explain that all women shared the responsibilities of the household and that she would expect that of me. Ms. Agnes proudly announced that she would take me on a tour of the house.

She was called away to do something and she let me know she would be right back. I sat in the room and for the first time in a long time, I felt protected. I felt as though all of the hurt and pain was going to be over. No more abuse from Carlos. For a moment, I worried that he would find me, but I promised myself that I would go by the rules and lay low until it was time for me to be on my own.

Ms. Agnes returns to the room where I was sitting. "Amiyah, come with me, sweetie, and let me show you around and show you your room."

We walked down a hall and standing around were lots of women talking. I could hear kids laughing and playing, and babies crying. She introduced me to the ladies in the hallway as the new lady in the house. We came to the room where I was to stay. In there at the time was one other single woman. Ms. Agnes introduced us and left the room so I could get comfortable. The room had two bunk beds, two desks, a phone, and one big dresser. I didn't have anything to unpack. I only had the clothes on my back and I wasn't going back home to get any clothes.

My roommate's was name Heather. She didn't say too much. I noticed the burn marks on her face and arms, but I didn't want to stare at her. She was sitting down on her bed writing in what appeared to be a journal.

"Hello," Heather spoke. I spoke back and began having a conversation. Heather told me how nice the home and the women were. Grinning a bit, she then told me about Ms. Agnes. "Ms. Agnes is very stern, but she is here to help," Heather mentioned to me. She went on to say that Ms. Agnes was very motherly to all of the ladies treated us as her own daughters.

I was happy to hear that I was at a safe place and could start a beginning of a new life for me. I walked over, bent down, gave Heather a hug, and let her know how much I appreciated her kindness and welcoming me into the home.

Heather had left the room for some reason. At that time, I decided to give my parents a call to let them know that if Carlos was to call looking for me to tell them they hadn't heard from me. However, I told my parents that I was okay, and that I went away and took some time for myself. My parents agreed. I never told my parents where I was, why I was there, or what I was doing there. Ms. Agnes made it clear that we were not to let anyone know of our whereabouts.

Ms. Agnes returned into the room where I was. She asked me to have a seat, and she sat at the desk while I sat on one of the beds. Ms. Agnes discussed with me all the opportunities there were out there for me and the different speakers she would have to help us grow and be on our own. Handing me a journal on her way out the door, Ms. Agnes lastly stated, "Now, Amiyah, I do request to all the women, as they come aboard, write their future plan. I want to know what is it that you expect to learn from being here. I want to know your goals and although it's hard to talk about, I would like to know why you decided to stay with your boyfriend as long as you did and why you decide to leave. After you are finished, bring it to my room and we will discuss it."

I agreed with her and after she left the room, I sat at one of the desks in the room, took a deep breath, and began writing in my journal. Talking about my situation was nothing I preferred to do, but since Ms. Agnes was there to help, I thought it would be helpful. Not in any particular order, I wrote that my goals were to build up my self esteem and go back to school to get a degree in Business Law. I wrote that I wanted to be able to live again, smile again, and not be angry at the world. I wanted to love and trust again. I wanted to learn how to go out in the world, work, and pay my own bills.

As far as Carlos, my boyfriend, I stayed with him for so long because I was dependent on him. He worked and he paid the bills. He did everything. I couldn't leave and make it on my own without him. I tried before, but always came back. I needed help, so that was why I was there. I was fed up and ready to leave him.

In Ms. Agnes' home was my escape. I figured I could get the support and help I need from there. I closed my journal, held it close to my heart, and got up from the desk. It was starting to get later in the night, so I wanted to get the paper to Ms. Agnes right away. I walked out the door to find Ms. Agnes' room.

Walking down the hallway looking around, I ran into a Latina lady that appeared to be in her late twenties. She had two small kids with her. I guess she noticed that I was looking for someone. Approaching me, she told me her name.

"Hi, I'm Connie." I told her my name and I let her know that it was nice meeting her. "Are you looking for someone?" she questioned.

I explained to her that I was looking for Ms. Agnes' room. She told me that her room was two doors down on the right from where we were standing. I thanked Connie for her help and knocked on Ms. Agnes' door.

"Come on in," I heard her voice behind the door. I opened the door. "Hi, Amiya."

Handing Ms. Agnes my paper, I spoke back. I knew that she wanted to discuss my goals further, so I started to get a little nervous and felt as if an anxiety attack was coming on. I never liked talking about my domestic violence situation, it wasn't anything I was proud to mention, mostly because I was embarrassed and also because no one never understood.

"Have a seat. I am glad you came back to see me. Some women, although being their first day here, would have left by now. The fact that you made it the whole day shows your determination to be a survivor of domestic violence," Ms. Agnes said proudly.

I sat in a chair across from her with tears streaming down my face because finally, I felt that someone was listening to me, someone understood me and had faith in me. That was all I ever wanted was for someone to listen to me. I didn't need the negativity, I didn't need anyone to bash my man, because no matter what he did, he was my man and I was going to protect him because I was his woman.

Ms. Agnes glanced over my paper and went on with asking me questions. "What would you say to other women in your situation that wants to get out of an abusive relationship but doesn't know how?"

I dropped my head and cried more than I ever had when I was with Carlos and when he was abusing me. I guess it was the fact that I felt safe. I felt it was okay to trust Ms. Agnes with my emotions and feelings. I muttered a sound of anger. I clutched my hands together, lift my head up, and answered her question.

"I would tell other women in domestic violence situations that are trying to get out that it's not their fault. I would let them know that they are someone to live for. At times, I know that others may not feel that people understand them. However, you can find support groups for women that are experiencing or has experienced the same situations. It's not okay to be a victim of domestic violence. You can live again." I went on to tell Ms. Agnes that I would want them to know that there were early signs and not to avoid them. The signs could be as "innocent" as a little push or as much as a fist in your mouth, but they were all signs you should never ignore, they would get worse.

Ms. Agnes stood up and motioned for me to stand up with her. She wiped the tears from my eyes and told me that I was somebody and I would survive. I thanked her, opened the door, and began walking back to my room.

As I was walking, I began thinking that I hadn't felt this happy in a long time and from that point on, I knew it was the beginning of a new life. I may have been beaten down, but I was standing up right there right then for myself and all the other victims of domestic violence.

§§§§§§

In memory of all victims and survivors of Domestic Violence.

As I wrote my short story *Someone To Live For*, without any question or thought I wanted to dedicate my story to those who are victims and survivors to Domestic Violence. My story was not about any specific or real situation. My story along with the other great authors who contributed to this anthology is to break the silence of Domestic Violence. Everyone that knows of someone in this type of situation is affected. You may be a victim's best friend, parent, sister, brother, child, classmate, neighbor, and so on. All are affected and involved. No one should go through this vicious, emotional, physical, or verbal situation however it happens, and some victims keep it silent for a reason of their own. If you know someone who is in a Domestic Violence relationship, it's up to you to listen and not judge.

My prayers go out to all victims' family and those they left behind.

§§§§§§

Nichole Payton resides in Northern VA with her two sons. She currently works for the Federal Government with not a lot of time on her hands with spending time with her family, friends, and working a full time job. She always seems to find time for her gift of writing. Nichole contributed the short story *Someone to Live For* in this anthology. She is the co-author of a short story titled *Double Shot of Mocha, Please* in an anthology titled *Tasty Temptations* with My Time Publications. She is soon to publish her debut novel *Shifted* with My Time Publications as well.

If It Isn't Love...
Shay

CHAPTER ONE

To say I was in love was beyond a doubt, overshadowing my true feelings. I was obsessed. I needed it. I wanted it. Every second, every minute, every hour. I had to have it. No, matter the cost or the price. The love was a drug. I would call it my morphine. No, better yet, it was my heroin. I was addicted to what I had experienced. Never in my life had I felt so completely absorbed in one person. Even when the beatings started, I did not give a fuck about what it was doing to me physically or mentally. I knew though it was going to come a time when I had to face facts. This shit was crazy and it had to stop! Let me tell you my story.

****

"Excuse me! Miss! Miss!" I turned around and stopped dead in my tracks. "Boy, do you move fast! I had to take two stairs at a time just to catch you," he said breathlessly. "You dropped this." He handed me a file folder that fell out of my briefcase. I looked over the man that stopped me. "Where are you off to in such a hurry?" he asked.

"Marketing Magic...upstairs," I managed to say.

I was ashamed at the way I looked when I caught a glimpse of my reflection in the mirror. My auburn brown, shoulder length hair had fallen out of the ponytail I had it in and was laying wildly around my shoulders. My makeup was nonetheless perfect, and sweat was running down my face.

"I'd be happy to assist you in carrying your things," he said.

He took my things from me and smiled. I smiled back, it was all I could do. He was breathtaking. I was talking the type of man other women had to stop and stare. Chocolate in color, dimples, low hair cut, and white teeth. He put me in the mind of the actor, Idris Elba, only a few inches shorter.

I let him guide me down to my office, all the while curious if he had a woman in his life. I searched his ring finger for tan lines or even a ring, but none existed. I let my hope diminish that he would find me attractive when I caught a glimpse of my figure in the glass doors near the entrance of my office. The navy blue pinstripe, Donna Karen pant suit I was wearing was hugging all of my rolls. I was not an ugly woman by far, but being a size eighteen was not the easiest when all you ever saw on TV were women who were a size four or smaller. I had hips, breasts, stomach, and a huge butt. I had to tell myself to let go of any chance of ever being with him.

"Well, here you are, safe and sound at your office." He handed me my stuff, flashed a heartwarming smile, and walked away down the hall.

Damn he was fine! I watched him walk away until he was out of sight. I walked through my office door and realized I forgot to get his name. I shook my head at my stupidity and went on about my day.

I found myself constantly thinking about him. I went to work every day for a month praying I would see him again, when one day I spotted him sitting outside of my office. It was somewhat strange, but I paid it no mind. I was just happy to see him again. My approach was apprehensive at first, as I was unsure of what he would want from me.

"Hello," was all I could manage to say. When he looked at me, he smiled.

"Well, hello. If it isn't Speedy Gonzales, how are you?" he said.

I laughed nervously. "I'm good. My name is Story. Story Reed. I did not give you my name when you helped me some time ago."

He stood there staring at me. I was awe struck and tongue tied all at the same time. I started praying my lips would move and some words would come out. I knew I had to look stupid just standing there.

"Story, is it? Now, that is quite a name. One could never forget that." He smiled again. Damn! His smiles were contagious and I felt the corners of my mouth turning up into a smile to match his. "My name is Silas Mason." He extended his hand out to me. "I came by to ask if you would you like to have lunch with me today?"

I had to look at him to make sure he was talking to me. "Sure, I would love to."

"Great, then meet me at Applebee's at about 12:30."

"Ok."

I went back to my desk very excited. He wanted to date me! I tried hard to get through the rest of the morning. When noon came, I jetted to the bathroom to check my hair in the mirror. I straightened my blouse and was glad I wore my girdle underneath it to keep my stomach from looking so swollen.

I made it to the hallway at 12:15 and applied a bit of my chocolate, MAC lip gloss to my lips before walking to my car. Lunchtime traffic was a bit heavy on the avenue, causing me to take a different route. When I finally arrived at the restaurant, I noticed Silas waiting for me outside on the bench. It was exactly 12:35. I exited my car and began walking toward him, hoping my girdle would not ride up as I walked.

"Hey, sorry I'm late, traffic was a beast."

"Just don't let it happen again."

The tone in his voice made me feel bad for my tardiness, even if it was just by a few minutes. He smiled and handed me a dozen roses. All I could do was smile.

"I grabbed them from the flower shop next door. I hope you like them.

I sniffed a rose and smiled. "I love them." I replied.

"Great! Now, come on, we only have an hour to eat." He opened the door for me and we went inside.

Sitting at the table with this man was truly a rewarding experience for me. I had not been on a real date in a very long time. Silas was so different. He was very particular about how his knife and fork were placed on the table, and very strict about

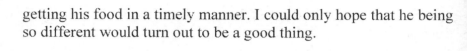

getting his food in a timely manner. I could only hope that he being so different would turn out to be a good thing.

CHAPTER TWO

The instant attraction to Silas always kept me hungry for more. I did not think he understood just how absorbed in him I was becoming. I lost focus in my work and started slacking on my production. All I could think about was when the next time I would get to see Silas. After the day we had lunch, I visited with him in the building's cafeteria everyday on all of my breaks. He did not seem to mind my company. I started inviting him over to my house, and ignored the fact he never invited me over to his, leading me to believe that maybe he was married or taken. I did not care! I was so desperate for his attention that I was willing to share it with whomever he was dating. I took the liberty to find out all I could about him.

He told me he was thirty five years old and had never been married. He said he was an only child. I told him I also was an only child and that I was twenty nine years old. I let him know my mother was killed when I was sixteen and my father was absent my entire life, so I never knew who he was. I felt we had so much in common. He was so gentle in spirit and very attentive.

I never complained about him waiting for me everyday after work by my car or being outside of my office on every break and lunch I had. Silas made me laugh and I felt he really understood me as a woman. I just knew he was 'the one'. Other men I had dealt with either complained about my size or wanted to keep me as a booty call and nothing more.

After four months of dating, I began to worry about our relationship. He had yet to talk of being exclusive and I still had not been to his house. Silas became a part of my every day life, always being around whenever he knew where I would be. He would sometimes make a fuss if I did not tell him where I was going all the time, but I took that as he just wanted me to be safe.

"So, you mean to tell me this mofo still hasn't taken you to his house and is always around? Girl, be careful of that. It sounds fishy," my coworker, Nicole, said one day.

"Nicole, I don't think he means me no harm. He likes me a lot. I like him, too. It's nice to have someone always there for you."

"Not always! When do you get time to miss his ass if he always in your face?"

I just shook my head. I did not expect her to understand since she had been married twice before. Leaving work for lunch, I found Silas in his normal spot by my car.

"Story, I need to tell you something." Silas looked me in the eye. He had a look of worry on his face.

"What is it, babe?"

He looked around the parking lot again. "My job met today and they are eliminating my position from the company at the end of the week."

"So, you are getting fired?"

"Well, yes and no. My entire department got the axe due to cuts in the budget and some funding issues. There is no longer any money left to pay my staff and me."

"Oh wow! I am sorry to hear that. Do you need anything? Money? I have some money saved up I could give you." I looked at him and he was looking away. I truly felt bad for him. He turned to me suddenly as if he had a revelation.

"Marry me!" he said. I frowned and looked around to make sure I heard him incorrectly. "Well?" He was waiting on a response.

I knew I loved him. I loved him from the first moment I had bumped into him. Sure, we had only been dating four months, but how much time was needed to know if you wanted to be with someone? Without giving it a second thought, I responded.

"Yes! Yes I will marry you!"

He smiled the smile I loved so much. "I don't have a ring, but I can get you one today."

I was smiling and nodding my head. I did not really care about a ring. I was finally going to belong to someone! Me! The fat and lonely child that grew up by herself with nothing and one to call her own was finally going to belong to someone! He took my chin into his hand pulling my face close to him and gave me the softest most passionate kiss I had ever received.

We went back to work after lunch and I could not focus for the rest of the day. My heart was bouncing around at the thought of being Mrs. Silas Mason. He made me promise not to tell anyone until he put a ring on my finger. I tried so hard to contain my excitement, even bumping into some old woman in the hallway knocking all of her belongings to the floor.

"I'm so sorry," I said to her.

She smiled at me. "It's ok dear. You look very happy about something. God must be good to you," she said while gathering her things.

I looked around to make sure no one else was listening. I looked down at the woman and helped her pick up some of her papers. "I just got engaged!" I beamed.

"Congratulations!" She looked at my finger and I instantly regretted sharing that information with her. When she finally stood up, she extended her hand. "I'm Ms. Agnes. I am here to see a..." She stopped to look at a name on a piece of paper. "Ms. Story Reed about a silent marketing project I'm working on."

"I'm Story Reed. I apologize for practically knocking you down, Ms. Agnes, come right into my office so we can discuss your project."

I guided her to my office and offered her a seat. Ms. Agnes was a nice looking older woman in her sixties with long black hair. Even with the strands of gray, she looked good. She wanted to discuss how to get women whom were abused information about her home without being obvious. It took me less than two hours to formulate a plan. While we were going over some paperwork, I received a call.

"Ms. Reed, there is a Silas Mason out here to see you," the secretary said.

I smiled. "Tell him I am with a client and I'll be out in a minute."

"He says it's urgent."

Ms. Agnes looked at me and smiled. "Go on, dear. If you need to excuse yourself, I can wait."

I smiled and walked out to the lobby. My mouth dropped open at the sight of Silas standing there in a black tuxedo with what looked to be four dozen roses. There was a young gentle men standing next to him.

"I'm sorry I couldn't wait. This is my friend, Ross. He is here as a favor. Go on, Ross, do your thang, brother."

I had no words as more roses were coming in different vases, held by different people. My coworkers were all smiling at me as if they knew something that I did not. The person named Ross started singing.

"*There will never come a day. You will ever hear me say. That I want and need to be without you. I want to give my all. Baby, just hold me. Simply control me. 'Cuz your arms, they keep away the lonlies. When I look into your eyes, then I realize, all I need is you in my life. All I need is you in my life. 'Cuz I never felt this way about lovin'. Never felt so good. Never felt this way about lovin'. It feels so good.*"

I was practically in tears after hearing my favorite Brian McKnight song. Silas walked over to me and got down on one knee. "I have never been more sure of what I am about to do. Story, I love you. I knew the day I bumped into you it was meant to be. I cannot see myself being without you. Will you do me the honor of being my wife?"

Tears were flowing down my cheeks as I watched him open up a ring box and show me a one carat solitaire diamond ring. He slid it on my finger. I felt myself began to hyperventilate.

"Well, answer him, child." I turned around and Ms. Agnes had come out into the lobby.

"Yes...yes. Yes...yes!" I almost knocked Silas over as I hugged him tighter than I ever had. He kissed me softly on the lips and held me tight. It was the best day of my life.

CHAPTER THREE

"I don't get why you haven't been to this man's house yet. He sounds like he's hiding something," my friend, Marlon, said.

I set a glass of Moscato down on the table before looking at him. Marlon and I had been friends for a couple of years. We met when he handled a case for my office. He was an older, gay man, so he usually schooled me on the men I dated.

"He's not hiding anything. I just think that maybe he does not want me to see how he is living just yet. Maybe he is messy."

Marlon took a sip from his glass and laughed. "Believe that if you want to, girl. That man is hiding something. How convenient that he loses his job, asked you to marry him, and you do not know anything about him but what he tells you. Add to that the fact that he is always around is a bit unnerving."

Before I could respond, I heard a knock at the door. "That must be him now," I said.

Marlon shook his head. "See what I mean? Always around! That is not healthy."

I walked to the front door. When I opened it, Silas was standing there looking as good as ever in his Polo shirt and blue jeans.

"Hey you," he said before smiling and giving me a kiss. He handed me a teddy bear and a long stem rose. It had been exactly a month since he came to my office and proposed. We had yet to set a date and even though I asked him to move in, he refused.

"Hey, baby, come on in. I'd like you to meet someone." He froze at the door. I frowned. "Is that a problem?" I asked.

"No."

I dismissed the weird way Silas was acting and took his hand and led him into the kitchen. "Marlon, this is Silas Mason. Silas, this is my friend, Marlon..."

Silas cut me off in midsentence. "Marlon Williams, you are an attorney, right?" Silas extended his hand eagerly.

Marlon had a funny look on his face as he took his hand. "Yes, that's right."

"It's so nice to finally meet you!"

"Wish I could say the same."

I gave Marlon a look and was glad Silas did not hear him. Marlon would not look me in the eyes, which really disturbed me. There was a brief silence. Marlon pushed back his chair to get up.

"Well, Story, I'm going to get out of here and let you two love birds have some...alone time." He gave Silas a look. "Nice meeting you, Silas."

"Likewise, Marlon."

"I'll walk you to the door," I said.

Marlon looked back over my shoulder to see if Silas was listening. "Story, I love you like my sister. You know that, right?" I nodded my head. "Well, when I say do not marry that man, I mean do not marry that man!"

He gave me a hug before exiting down my driveway to his car. I had no understanding of what had just occurred and did not give it any further thought. I went back into the kitchen and saw Silas standing at my sink. I walked up to him and put my breast on his back hugging him around his waist.

"So, how are you friends with Marlon Williams?"

"He worked on a case for my office and we went out for drinks one night and hit it off as friends." I tried to move my hands down to his thighs.

"When were you going to tell me you had a male friend?"

He threw me completely off as he moved my hands from his thighs. "I told you about Marlon before. You don't remember?"

"No, I don't!"

"Is that a problem?"

"Yes. My woman is not supposed to have any male friends unless she discusses it with me first!"

I pondered what he said. "I didn't think it would be a problem. Marlon is also my attorney."

"So, are you fucking your attorney?"

"What! No, never!"

His choice of words really had me perplexed since I rarely heard him cuss. I tried to hug him to get his mind off the matter, but he pushed me off him. "You know what, Story, I think you are lying. I saw how he looked at you before he left. As if he was sending, you eye signals. Y'all probably got one in before I came by!"

"No, Silas, you are being ridiculous! Now, please, let's just drop it!" I placed his hand on one of my breasts, hoping to distract him. He looked at me as if seeing me for the first time and turned his nose up. He snatched his hand away from my breast.

"Story, please, stop lying to me! I love you, but I can't have you lying to me."

I started to grow frustrated because I did not understand where it was going. "I'm not lying to you! You have to believe me! You can call Marlon back over here right now and ask him! He will tell you we are just friends!" I wanted this conversation to end.

"If I find out it's something else, I'm gone beat your ass."

I frowned for a second before immediately dismissing the threat. I knew he was just jealous and that he was only talking crazy for the moment. Once again trying to change the subject, I put his hand on my butt and wrapped my arms around his neck.

"Kiss me, please. I missed you all day."

He snatched his hand away from me and backhanded me in the face. The pain stung. I grabbed my cheek and looked at him in horror. My natural reaction was to hit him back, but I refrained from doing so.

"What the hell is your problem?" I screamed.

"You! You are my problem. Ask your little attorney friend to kiss you! Here I am patiently waiting on your fat ass to give me some pussy, and all along you been giving it out to your little friend."

"Silas, that's not true!" I was going to have to reveal Marlon's secret to him to make him believe me. "Marlon likes men. He is gay!"

Silas stood there processing what I had told him. "The biggest attorney in the city is gay? Wow!"

I held my hand to my cheek, still trying to digest everything that just happened. I heard the words "fat ass" echoing in my head. I felt the tears spill onto my cheeks and could not do anything more but stand there in shock. Silas looked at me and shook his head.

"I'm so sorry, Story. I do not know what got into me. I did not mean to overreact. Oh my God, please forgive me!" He started to kiss my face, my lips, and my cheek where he hit me. "Please, forgive me," he said again.

He kissed my neck and began to suck on it gently. My girl downstairs woke up instantly. I wanted to tell him to get out, but the hold he had on me was too strong. My mother was probably rolling over in her grave. She was the one who told me if a man hit you once, he will hit you again. This was different though. I wanted to be with this man. He did apologize for hitting me. I knew it was just a slip up. We all made mistakes, right?

He continued to kiss me while letting his hands roam over my body. He undid the buttons on my shirt and pulled my breasts free from my bra. He licked each nipple hungrily while caressing other parts of my body. I was on fire. I needed him. I wanted to feel him. He pulled my pants down and for the first time, I forgot to be embarrassed about my size. Silas kissed my stomach before pulling me down on the kitchen floor. He placed his face between my thighs and licked every piece of my being until I felt I could take no more. When he was done tasting me, he slipped his manhood inside of me. At first, I thought I heard fireworks. It was the best feeling I had felt in a very long time. The nagging feeling in the back of my mind told me I was making a big mistake, but the love Silas was giving me on that kitchen floor clouded every negative thought I had. He made love to me like a soldier who had been away at war, or a prisoner who had served a life sentence and was finally out. I knew there was only one conclusion. I was obsessed!

CHAPTER FOUR

"Girl, what the hell is his fucking problem? Why did he hit you? Do you need me to come over there? You know I will! Story, this is serious!"

I was on the phone with Marlon. "No, I don't need you to come over. It was just an accident. He apologized repeatedly."

"It was just an accident? Hitting a cat with a car is an accident. Being slapped in the face is not. Add to the fact that he called you a fat ass! Child, you really need to think about this."

"He is right. My ass is fat. I need to lose some weight. I mean, he stays in shape and works out all the time, so why can't I?"

I heard Marlon sigh. "Story, seriously, is this man that important? He isn't worth the bullshit. I don't think you really know this man like you think you do."

I paused to think about what he said until I heard keys at my front door. "I have to go, Marlon. He is here. I'll call you later."

"What? Do not tell me you gave this man keys to your house! Girl, you are crazy! If he touches you again, I will make him wish he never touched you in the first place! Tell him to step to a man with that bullshit."

I hung up the phone quickly and ran to the kitchen to grab the plate of meatloaf, mashed potatoes, and green beans; I had made Silas for dinner. After we made love, he stayed the night and made love to me again the next morning. I asked him once again to move in with me and he surprisingly agreed. I wanted to wake up next to him and get used to doing so before we were married. When Silas came in the house, he looked at me strangely.

"Who were you on the phone with?"

"What? No one, I made your favorite food, meatloaf and mashed potatoes!"

I watched as he glanced around the kitchen as if he were looking for something. He did not even pay attention to the plate on the table. He walked over to the fridge grabbed the bottle of Moscato, popped the cork, and poured the wine into a glass from the cupboard.

"I'm not hungry," he said, and then proceeded to walk away with the glass in his hand. I walked into the living room where I found him on the couch watching TV.

"Baby, what's wrong?"

He drew in a deep breath and then exhaled. "Look, Story, I know I agreed to move in with you, but I think I might be making a mistake. You do not really know who I am. I may not be the man you really need in your life right now." He took a sip from his glass.

"No, don't say that! You are what I need! I do not want to be with anyone else. Is it my weight? I promise I will start working out. I will join a gym. I will run with you in the morning. I'll do anything." I ran over to the couch and got on my knees in front of him. "I need you in my life. You have to understand that. I don't have anyone else."

Silas looked at me and took another sip from his glass. "Look at you! Why are you on your knees?"

I got very desperate. I could not imagine him leaving me. I got up and sat on the couch. "Please, Silas, tell me what to do to make things better. I promise I will be the woman you need me to be. I promise!"

He laughed at me. "Wow, you are a fat trip for real. You that serious, huh?" He sat the glass of wine down on the table beside the couch. "Let's go ahead and get married. Forget about setting a date, forget the whole bells and whistles. Let's just do it this weekend!"

In my head, I knew I should have asked why he was rushing it, but after a second, it did not matter. I lost my mother, had no father, so why not. "That's great. I will call Marlon and some of my coworkers. We can do it in the backyard."

Silas frowned. "What do you need to call them for?"

"Baby, we are getting married. It is the most important event in anyone's life. I just wanted to share it with the people who have been there for me."

Silas picked up his glass and swallowed what was left of the Moscato. He poured another glass and looked at me a long time before speaking. "I said let us do it. That meant just you and me. We do not need anyone else there. This is our decision. You can tell everyone after we are married."

****

We decided to get married down at the lake that Saturday. Silas found a friend of his that was a preacher to marry us. It was a simple ceremony; just the preacher, Silas, and me. I really wished I could have had the dream wedding every girl dreamed about, but at least I had the love of my life. We chose not to go on a honeymoon since Silas was currently unemployed.

Some weeks later, his drinking began to pick up and he was always drunk. There were times when he would call me names and then apologize for it the next morning. He never wanted me to leave to go anywhere, so my life began to center around him and only him. The one time I went to the mall, I just happened to bump into Marlon there. Silas must have followed me, again, and flipped out on me. He snapped off on me for the first time in public in the middle of the food court. When he approached me, he reeked of alcohol.

"Do you know what time it is?" he growled at me. I looked at my watch. It was only half past five o'clock. "Why aren't you at home making my dinner?"

"I was at work, Silas, you know that. I stopped here to grab a few things."

"Naw, bitch. You were with that mufucka I told you to stay away from. Weren't you?"

"No! Why are you always so insecure?"

He grabbed me by the arm and led me to the parking lot where my car was. People were staring at us as he pulled me through the mall like a child. When we arrived at my Honda Civic, he pushed me to the ground and hit me in the face. The pain from the blow was unbearable. I grabbed my face and felt something wet on my hands. I looked down at my hand and there was blood.

"I saw you with your so called friend once again. I knew you were fucking around on me."

"No, I am not. Please, you have to believe me!" My face was throbbing.

"Why didn't you tell me about your little mall adventure? Why do I have to follow you around to make sure you being truthful with me? As my wife, you have to get permission to go anywhere other than work from me first!"

Silas grabbed me by the neck and shoved me against the car. He wrapped his hands around my throat and squeezed. I felt the pressure in my head and my eyes felt like they were going to pop out the sockets. After what seemed like five minutes, but was really only a few seconds, he gave up and released me. I coughed and spat, gasping for air. People walked by looking and whispering, but no one said anything.

"You fat fucking bitch! You better be lucky I haven't killed you yet!" He walked away leaving me alone.

I began to sob uncontrollably. I had no understanding on why all this craziness was happening to me. Silas went from being sweet and loving to jealous and overprotective. I did everything he wanted me to. I knew I needed to leave, but I never did. I stayed put for the next six months.

CHAPTER FIVE

One day, I was feeling sick and knew my period was late. Silas had left the house to run errands. I was scared to go anywhere for fear he might follow me, draw the wrong conclusion, and beat me up again. I decided to go to the drug store and buy one of those home pregnancy tests. When I got into my car to leave, I noticed Ms. Agnes' marketing info on my front seat. I began to cry. It had to be a sign. Who would have thought I might have to use my client's service for myself? I pulled myself together and promised I would give her a call.

After peeing on the stick, I waited in the bathroom for the results. Looking in the mirror, I did not recognize the woman staring back at me. This woman was overweight, ugly, and weak with bruises on her face. When the test read positive, I waited for Silas to get home to tell him about my pregnancy.

I had committed myself to leave if he presented any danger to me and my unborn child. To my surprise, Silas was more than elated about my pregnancy and for a while, things seemed to turn around. He once again became the sweet and loving man I fell in love with.

Nine months later, we had a son that we named Lenox James Mason. He looked just like Silas, only lighter. Since I was of a mixed race, he picked up my light brown colored eyes and wavy hair. He was a very beautiful child and I loved him more than I loved Silas. It had been nine months since he had hit me. I figured it was just a phase and that everything would be OK from now on. Every marriage had problems, right?

Just when I thought things were looking up, they began to get that much worse. Silas started to act strange after I brought our son home from the hospital. He told me Lenox was too light skinned to be his and that he belonged to Marlon, who had a lighter complexion.

Marlon abruptly stopped talking to me after that day at the mall. When I thought Silas had stopped drinking because I did not see any more bottles, I realized he had picked up a new habit of snorting cocaine. I found the powdery substance in a small baggie in our drawer. I did what I saw them do on TV, putting my finger in the bag and running it along my gums. I felt an instant numbing sensation and knew it was true. I was devastated. I went into panic mode. I had recently made him a joint signer on my account after we were married and was afraid of what the balance would be when I checked it. I picked up the phone to dial the bank while I nursed my son.

"Your account balance is negative five thousand, six hundred dollars, and thirty nine cents. Your last deposit of…"

I slammed the phone down, causing Lenox to jump in my arms. He drained out my savings and the money to pay the mortgage. I did not know what to do. I had no money and a baby to take care of. I picked up the phone to call Marlon for a loan. Suddenly, Silas appeared out of nowhere.

"You stupid fucking bitch. You still talking to this nigga behind my back I see. I am going to teach you a damn lesson you will never forget," he growled at me as spit flew from his mouth.

Before I could get a word out, Silas tackled me in a football position, pushing me to the floor. Lenox rolled out of my arms and onto the floor. I tried to force myself to get up and run to my son who was screaming, with no effort. Silas hit me repeatedly. I remember trying to block my face from the blows, but it was like holding a paper towel to someone with a water hose. Eventually, everything was dark and the sounds of my baby crying were in the distance.

I awoke later to find I was still on the floor. Lenox was on the floor on his side suckling at my breast for dear life. He looked as if someone had placed him there. Every part of my body ached. I scooped my baby up in my arms and tried to move slowly without disturbing him. I could hear Silas downstairs on the phone with someone. I looked around for my purse and found it under the bed. Ms. Agnes' contact info jumped out at me. If I was going to leave, I had to leave now. I grabbed my cell phone, but then remembered that every time I used it Silas seemed to know whom I was talking with.

I found two quarters for a pay phone, grabbed a diaper from Lenox's diaper bag, and stuffed it inside my jeans. The sound of footsteps coming up the stairs caused me to freeze. I repositioned myself back where I was and placed Lenox in the same position. He continued to suck from my breast. I closed my eyes and pretended to be unconscious. I could smell must, liquor, and some other type of odor coming from Silas as he hovered over me.

"Yea, that's right, little man. Get all the milk you can 'cause this fat mother of yours been sucking all the food down just for you. Maybe you can help her burn some of these calories off." Silas erupted into a laugh. I held on to the tears that wanted to fall from my eyes. I watched out of one eye as he fell across the bed and seemed to pass out in a drunken stupor.

After waiting five minutes, I crawled on my hands and knees until I made it to the hallway with Lenox in my arms. I darted down the stairs, ignoring the pain coming from my body and headed for the front door. It was pouring rain outside. I looked around for my car, but it was gone. I decided to run down the street to the gas station, putting Lenox underneath my shirt. I made it to the pay phone and dialed Marlon with the first quarter. There was no answer. I pulled Ms. Agnes' info out and dialed her cell phone number.

"This is Ms. Agnes."

"Please, you have to help me. I have to get away from him."

"OK, calm down. What's your name, sweetie?"

"Story...Story Mason!"

There was a brief pause. "Oh my dear, where are you?"

I pulled Lenox closer to my chest. "I'm at the Mobile gas station on 5th and Clarke."

"I'll be right there. Go inside and wait for me."

"No, please. I do not want to alert him. He will hunt me down." I began to sob. "Please, just come get me." My knees started to feel weak. I saw what looked like Silas' black truck pulling into the station. "He's here, Ms. Agnes, I have to go!"

"Stay on the phone with me, Story…Story? Story, are you there? Oh dear God!"

CHAPTER SIX

When I saw that truck turn into that parking lot, I dropped the receiver to the phone and ducked down. I could hear the panic in Ms. Agnes' voice as she called my name repeatedly. I was sure if I picked up the phone he would see or hear me talking. He walked around that gas station as if he just knew I was there. It was as if he had a sensor on me. I cradled my son so close to my body, I thought I had suffocated him because he was so quiet. When I looked down, he was using my nipple as his pacifier and had fallen asleep, oblivious to anything that was going on. I hid my behind a garbage can in the rain, waiting for God to perform a miracle for me. Silas walked around the station several times.

"I don't see her," Silas said.

"She's here. She just called me from that pay phone over there."

My heart broke in a million pieces. That was the sound of Marlon's voice. I wanted to believe I was hallucinating when I saw him get out of Silas' truck.

"Why the hell you beat her up? I'll never understand. I told you to leave her alone!"

Silas laughed. "You are fucking hilarious, captain save- a-hoe! Do you know she told me you were gay? My brother, the big shot attorney, gay! "

"You know I'm not gay!"

"Oh I know, and I don't give a fuck!" Silas took a swig from a silver flask. "As usual, you punked out on the pussy. You saw a beautiful woman and instead of taking a chance, you wanted me to treat her bad so she could keep running to you for comfort and then you would put your moves on her. Here is where you messed up, brother. Gay men do not just turn straight over night, so there was no way she would have accepted you anyhow. Now, give me my money!"

"You don't get any money. You were not supposed to marry her, beat her up, and then impregnate her. She's no good to me now!"

I tried hard to block out the information I was hearing. It had to be some sick joke. I made a move to adjust my position behind the garbage, which made a noise. Marlon turned in my direction. He looked me dead in the eyes and dropped his head. He knew I heard the conversation. I felt the tears running down my face.

"Do you see her over there?" Silas called out.

Marlon looked at me again mouthed the words "sorry" and turned around and left. "No, she's not here. Let's just go."

I waited until they both got back into the truck and drove off.

****Going Forward****

When Ms. Agnes finally arrived at the gas station, she took me to her home. My emotions were all over the place because I had no understanding of what had just happened.

"Count yourself lucky that man did not kill you. What they did to you was sick, but it is all over now. You are safe."

"I loved him. I gave him everything and it was all a lie. It was all a lie." I started to cry. Ms. Agnes placed her arms around me and hugged me. My heart was broken. I felt worse than I did when the beatings occurred. The betrayal from the two people I cared about the most hurt worst than any fist against my face. She showed me to a room that had two bunk beds along with various toys.

"Dinner is served at five, and there are some clothes you will find in the closet that can fit you," Ms. Agnes said. She closed the door behind her and left me alone to my extremely loud thoughts.

I sat Lenox down on one of the bunk beds and dried him off with a dry towel. I rummaged through the clothes in the closet and found nothing but some old jeans and t-shirts. Some of the jeans were very outdated. I found a pair in a size sixteen and knew they would fit. I slipped them on just to see and to my surprise, they did not fit. They were too big. I grabbed a size fourteen and they fit perfectly. I laughed to myself because I had finally lost weight and did not even notice. As I was pulling a t-shirt over my head, another woman walked into the room with two small kids. From the bags under her eyes, she looked exhausted. Her kids hid behind her as she closed the door. She was a Latina with very beautiful skin.

"I'm Maritza Lopez, and these are my children," she said to me.

I stuck my hand out. "Nice meeting you, Maritza. My name is Story, and that's my son, Lenox James, on the bed."

She sat down on the opposite bed. "Story, that's a pretty name. So, what's your story...Story?" She giggled at the pun.

I smiled and giggled a little. Her kids found the toys in the room and began to play.

"It's crazy and very twisted is what I can say. The man I thought loved me did not. I only got two years to tell you about though."

"Wow, is that all, Mami? I have twelve years on you, so you go first!"

I looked at her and she smiled. I knew we would get along just fine. I picked up Lenox and held him close in my arms. I curled my feet underneath me and began to tell her my story.

§§§§§§

Shay Gray (formerly known as Shalya "Shay" Crape) is a published author of a novel titled *Truth Hurts* through Amiaya Entertainment. She has also contributed to three anthologies with this current one being her fourth. *The Good Ol' Days* in *Social Security* through Amiaya Entertainment. *Twisted Love* in *That's the Way Love Goes* through My Time Publications. *Imitation of Life* in *Street Vices* through Take Over Publishing. Shay has also ventured out in her writing abilities. She joined a group called **Brothas & Sistas After Dark a.k.a BSAD Live:** A show featuring sketches, interviews, & live talk show discussions around relationships. You can check out some of her work via Youtube/bsadmedia.

She is currently at work on several projects to include writing a script for a short film titled, *ALANA*, along with Park Hill Films, and the completion and release of her second and third novels to be released under her own publishing company, Pink Shade Publications coming in 2011.

Trophy Wife
Leila Jefferson

Perfection

My breath got caught my throat when my eyes shot open and I saw it was four thirty seven in the morning. I was seven minutes late. Quickly and quietly, I shot out of the bed, made my side, and dashed to the bathroom. I plugged the plug in the socket to begin heating the rollers, and then I brushed my teeth, cleansed and moisturized my face, and turned on the shower. Before getting in the shower, I made a beeline to the baby's room to make sure Jordyn was OK. Seeing she was sound asleep, I ran back to the shower and cleansed myself with his favorite peach scented body wash, the scent I had grown to hate, then dashed out the shower to roll my hair and start breakfast.

He had to have fresh squeezed orange juice, three oranges every day, and the juice had to be strained at least three times to ensure there was no pulp and definitely no seeds. He liked a bowl of oatmeal with seven raisins mixed in, exactly seven every time. I prepared two sunny side up eggs and put the toast in the toaster. I had to watch that toast, if it wasn't toasted to his liking, things could get ugly.

After setting breakfast on the tray as if it were a display in a fancy restaurant, I snatched the rollers out of my hair and quickly did my makeup and fingered out the curls. I grabbed one of my dresses out the hall closet, put it on quickly, and took the tray to the room, displaying a perfect Miss America smile. As if on cue, Kenneth stretched, sat up, and lazily rubbed his eye.

"Good morning, honey. Breakfast is ready," I said in barely above a whisper as I kept my head toward the floor and walked over to him.

"Where are your shoes?" he asked evenly.

Shit, in the rush to make sure everything was perfect, I had forgotten to put them on. "I apologize. I was up with the baby and the alarm..."

He knocked the tray from my hand. My heart beat fast as he got up from the bed and stood in front of me. Like an animal, he slowly sniffed me. With his finger on my chin, he slightly raised my head. "I'm in a good mood today. Have things right by the time I get out the shower and get dressed."

"Thank you," I whispered gratefully. I finally exhaled when he closed the door to the bathroom. "Get it together, Misa," I whispered as I moved quickly to rectify the wrongs.

I scrubbed my face in the hall bathroom. I knew my makeup wasn't up to par. I cleaned the spilled food in the room, reapplied my makeup, and went to the kitchen to make breakfast again. I pulled out a red Prada dress and matching slingbacks. I pulled my hair in an updo, sprayed the peach body spray, and got breakfast on the table just as Kenneth was turning the corner to the kitchen.

He looked me over from head to toe. I always had to be picture perfect. He had wined and dined me in the beginning, and swept me off my feet. He wanted a trophy wife, and I was more than willing to be that. I had no idea what I was getting myself into.

Prey Spotted

I was at a fundraiser where the plates cost $1000 each having dinner with the most boring man I had ever met. He spent the entire time talking about himself and his job as a lawyer. I smiled and nodded, pretending to be interested as I tuned him out. I took a sip of Merlot and glanced in the direction of someone marvelous. He looked confident and in charge. In five seconds, I was able to tell he had on a tailor made Armani suit with Armani shoes that looked like he had just purchased them. He was money, and I wanted to know him. He caught me checking him out, and raised his glass in an imaginary toast. I blushed as I raised my glass in return.

"Do you know him?" my date asked, snapping me out of my thoughts.

"Oh, umm, I think my parents have had him over at dinner parties before," I lied.

To Calvin, I was part of the elite. He thought I came from a wealthy family because that was what I told him. I told him my dad worked on Wall Street and I was in the west coast for school. Truth was, I had never lived anywhere but the Bay Area. Hell, I didn't even go to college. I studied the rich and famous though. It was my calling to be a part of them, and I was determined to make it happen. I had dated a few dope boys, but they didn't live the life I had always dreamed of. I wanted to be someone's trophy wife. I wanted maids and cooks, and to be taken out to lavish restaurants all the time. I wanted my closet to be huge and filled with top of the line designers.

I had dated a few guys that were up to par in the financial department, but they seemed to have wives. How was I to become a trophy wife when they were already someone's husband? But, I did enjoy being trophy mistress, receiving my share of expensive gifts and a few vacations. Those gifts helped me step my game up and mingle in the crowds I wanted to be in. I would basically use whatever information I could get from whatever guy I was seeing to know where I needed to be. When I met Calvin, I was at a New Year's Eve party held in the hills of San Francisco. Although my 'boyfriend' was taking his wife, he felt bad for leaving me alone on New Year's Eve and made sure I could attend the party. He was hoping we'd sneak off and I'd give him a quickie, but I met Calvin and he had my attention most of the night. He was boring then as well, but I wanted to show Doug's ass a lesson.

Anywho, I needed to know who he was. As the announcer began to introduce the guest speaker, I was surprised to see him smile a modest smile at all the great things that were being said, then he got up from his seat and headed toward the podium. When his name was called, it sounded so familiar, but I knew I would remember someone as fine as him if I had met him before.

Although I paid no attention to what he was talking about, I was mesmerized as he spoke so eloquently and commanded everyone's attention. It was amazing how everyone in the room hung onto his every word. I had to meet him. He had to be mine.

Once everyone was up mingling, I tried to get into his circle without being too obvious. My date was still going on and on about himself, and I still hadn't heard a word he said until he asked, "Would you like to go to my place for a nightcap?"

If he had asked that question anytime before 'he' caught my eye, I would have said yes. The Louboutins and Gucci dress I had on were compliments of him, and I had planned on thanking him nicely. He was boring, but he was fine, he had money, and he wasn't married.

I let out a fake cough. "I'm not feeling too well. I think I should just go home and lie down," I answered, giving him an apologetic look.

"Oh no, I knew you should have worn a jacket. I'll go say goodbye to Kenneth and we can leave immediately."

Kenneth? Kenneth? Where had I heard that name before? Snap! My man! I quickly ditched the fake sick look, and took out my compact to freshen my lip gloss and made sure my face was straight. *Game time, Misa.*

"Kenneth, great speech tonight," Calvin said as he shook Kenneth's hand.

"You know they should have had you up there. I'm an amateur," Kenneth said with a wide smile. He looked my way. "And, what a lovely guest. You've come a long way since Oakland Tech, Jennifer, and even more beautiful than I remember."

I was confused and I knew my face showed it. I cleared my throat. I hadn't been Jennifer for years. "Umm, you have me mistaken for someone else." I couldn't have known him, I would have never forgotten that face. My mind raced through classmates from high school. I had no idea who he was.

"Misa here is from New York, Kenneth. She's here going to college at Berkeley." Calvin pulled me closer to him, almost in a territorial type fashion.

"My apologies, Misa. They say everyone has a twin, and Jennifer Powell is definitely yours. We went to Oakland Tech together, I was the nerdy guy back then." He let out a slight chuckle.

I searched my memory bank for a Kenneth. *No way!* I thought. The only Kenneth I could really remember was the dorkiest of dorks. He wore the thickest glasses I had ever seen and he had acne bad. I remembered he never matched and always looked like his clothes came from Goodwill. He was so in love with me. He always bought me Valentine's and birthday gifts, and would leave them at my locker. I never paid him any attention, I would tease him and his gifts in his face, and my friends and I would have the laughs of our life at his expense. My mouth fell open and I could tell that he knew I had finally remembered him.

Instead of busting me out, he said, "Well, I'm glad you could make it out, Calvin. And, Misa, enjoy your evening."

I didn't respond. "Misa's not feeling well. Matter of fact, I was just coming to say goodbye so I can get her home. I'll see you around," Calvin said and gave Kenneth another handshake.

I got in Calvin's Ferrari and laid my head back. Kenneth Wilson, the biggest nerd I had ever known, had turned into a handsome, eloquent, rich man. I noticed he had no ring, so I knew I would have no problems being his trophy wife.

Once I got home, I turned on my computer and looked Kenneth up on the Internet. I was amazed as learned he was more paid than I could have ever imagined. He had created some kind of software that had blown up. He did speaking engagements all over the world, he had tons of pictures of all the influential people he had met over the years, and he was still single. I rarely saw a woman with him. I studied him for hours, going to every link listed. I read article after article. That Musik song popped in my head because had I known the nerd would have been him, I sure would have been nicer back then. But, that didn't matter. I saw the way he looked at me. He was still in love, and I bet he had stayed single because he was waiting on me.

When I couldn't hold my eyes open any longer, I finally shut down my computer and went to sleep. I was finally going to live the life I had dreamed of my entire life.

Trophy Wife

Doing my homework, I found out Kenneth would be holding a seminar, something about power moves to be successful. I didn't care about that, I had only one thing in mind. I signed up for the seminar under a fake name. I didn't know if he personally went through the list of enrollees before hand, but I wanted to be a surprise.

Taking extra care to be at the top of my game, I took a long, soothing bath in peach scented bubble bath, used the peach body wash, and topped it off with the peach lotion. I had always loved peaches since I was a little girl. My momma made the best peach cobbler you would ever taste.

I precisely applied my makeup and allowed my curls to fall loosely. I put on black La Perla panties with a matching bra, and chose a simple Versace dress and matching shoes. I put on three carat tear drop earrings and a matching teardrop necklace. My boy toys had been awfully nice over the years, but I needed stability. I wanted to be able to have a black card in my name and shop 'til I dropped. I wanted the unlimited checking account. I was tired of gifts being dropped off for me. All the men had impeccable taste, but I wanted to buy what I wanted to buy.

Giving myself a satisfactory smile, I blew a kiss in the mirror and headed out to my BMW. I pulled up at the Marriot where the seminar was taking place, and went inside and had a seat. As Kenneth scanned the audience during the beginning of his speech, I saw him catch my eye and he stared at me a few seconds longer. Throughout his speech, he kept looking at me and smiling.

During the break, he came over to talk to me. "Hello, Jennifer, or should I call you Misa?" He chuckled. "How are you?"

I shook his hand. "It's Misa now. I'm well. How are you?"

"It's surprising to see you here," he said.

I moved a little closer. I was never one to beat around the bush and I was never one to be turned down. "I want you, Kenneth.

I know you always wanted me in school, well, here I am." I slipped him a keycard. "I'm in room 2746. When you're done here, I'll be waiting." I walked off without waiting for a response. I knew he'd be there.

I knew the seminar would be over at four. At four thirty, I heard the beep from the key card, and the door slowly opened. I lay across the bed with nothing but my La Perla to greet him. He stopped in his tracks, I could tell he was admiring me. After six years of being out of high school, I was still bad as could be. My perfect size six body held 38C breasts and an ass so round, Nelly made Apple Bottoms with me in mind. I had wiped off my old makeup and had a fresh layer applied as well as had touched up my hair. The scent of peaches was fresh in the air as I had laid out my web. To seal the deal, I took it a step further.

Not waiting on him to come closer to me, I slowly and seductively crawled out the bed, to the floor, and over to him. I licked my lips as I slowly raised myself to my knees. I could tell he loved the preshow because I could see his hardness through his pants, and boy was he packing. I wanted to kick myself for not giving him the time of day back in the day, but then I thought about the fact that I didn't have to go through all the awkward bullshit and 'sticking by my man 'til he made it' bullshit. I got him when he was ripe and rich, just my type. I undid his belt, button, and zipper slowly, then let his hardness sprang free. I licked my lips and gave him a blowjob that would put a prostitute to shame. The moaning he did turned me on even more, and when he grabbed a handful of my hair and guided my mouth just the way he liked it, I put in all the work I could.

"Move your hands," he demanded.

Without a second thought, I took my hand from the base of his dick and the other from his shaft. He put both his hands behind my head and fucked my mouth. I took it like a big girl and willed myself not to gag from his girth. I had never deep throated because I never wanted to put in that much work, but I wanted to make sure I did everything and more to get that ring on my finger. Just when I thought he had hit the back of my throat for the last time, he balled my hair up in his fists and held his length in my mouth as he came. I thought I was going to choke to death for a minute. The fluids were coming out so quick and it was so much. I held my breath for as long as I could, and when I began to feel lightheaded, he finally let me go. I breathed through my nose as I forced myself to swallow his jism. Not missing a beat, I got up and walked to the bed, unhooking my bra and dropping it, and taking off my panties on the way. I lay on the bed and spread eagle, inviting him in my hot box.

"I've fantasized about this moment for a long time," he said as he loosened his tie and walked toward me.

"No more fairytales, baby, this is real life," I said as I began to rub my clit. I watched him as he took off his expensive clothes and diamond cufflinks. I got wet adding up the figures in my head. When he was finally naked, I had a dollar intake of at least $15,000 from clothes and accessories.

He walked over to me and I couldn't take my eyes off him. Besides being paid, he was so fine. I could tell he spent a lot of time in the gym. He had a sculpted eight pack that stripper guys would kill for. The acne was long gone, his skin was smooth and blemish free. What they said was true, money made anyone look good. He kissed my thighs, up to my stomach, and then my breasts. As he sucked hard, he inserted himself inside of me in one rough push.

Look at scrubby Kenneth, trying to be forceful and shit, I thought as he gave me some straight from the Oakland hood, thug loving. He was everything I wanted. He was rich, fine, young, and could put it down. I closed my eyes and imagined being on his arm at fabulous events and taking exotic vacations. I imagined my maids and cooks and nannies taking care of the house and kids while I shopped all day and looked beautiful for my man. I came all over his dick as I saw myself swiping that black card in some expensive boutique in Paris. My life was changing, and I came again as he exploded inside of me.

"Wow, I can't believe I'm here with Jennifer Powell. Damn, my bad, Misa." Kenneth let out a chuckle.

I rubbed his chest. We were finally taking a break after he wore me out for over an hour. "You can call me anything you want."

"Now that I think about it, I'll stick with Misa. Jennifer wasn't too nice to me."

I suddenly felt like shit. "Hey, I'm sorry. I was young and..."

"Shhh. None of that matters now. It's a new day. We all did silly shit when we were young." I lowered my head because there wasn't really anything I could say. "So, Calvin your boyfriend?"

I laughed. "Boy, please. That was our first date and he bored the hell out of me. I'm single," I added to make it clear that I was available.

"What's up with the name change? And, from New York?" He chuckled.

"You know how it was back in the day. We were in the hood. I was hood rich dealing with the d boys, but I wanted more than that. I created a new persona to fit the life I was destined to live."

"I see. So, you're looking good, what have you been doing with yourself all these years?"

I didn't want to tell him I'd been bed bouncing and platinum digging, so I smiled at him and said, "Waiting on you."

He seemed to be content with that answer because he pulled me closer and kissed my forehead. "I'm here, so now what?"

"You tell me."

"Let's go to Vegas and spend some time together. I have a condo out there."

"That sounds great!" I said excitedly.

"Don't pack anything, I'll supply everything you need."

He had said the magic words. There was no way I was letting my platinum mine get away.

As I went to get in the shower, Kenneth pulled out his cell and made a call. I was used to that kind of stuff, he was making the arrangements for our getaway. I hummed to myself as I let the warm water soothe my body. I had maxed out my card getting the room, but I was sure I'd be able to get Kenneth to pay the bill. My $2500 limit was probably coins to him. I had a few other cards maxed out, and the rent on my loft was due. I had been slipping. I usually had my bills paid, but the last few months hadn't been good to me boy toy wise. Kenneth came at just the right time. Hell, maybe I could give up that condo and move in with him.

As I was deep in my fantasy, Kenneth joined me in the shower. He picked me up, had me against the wall, and fucked me hard. I licked and sucked on his neck and chest, imagining a big diamond ring on my finger. We would have a big ass wedding and I'd invite all the stank bitches from school to rub it in their faces. We'd go on a month long honeymoon and travel the world. He'd make love to me over and over until I got pregnant and had a kid, that way, if something ever went wrong or he tried to trade me in for a younger model, I'd have a big ass child support check and alimony to take care of me.

"Ahh, I'm about to cum!" Kenneth yelled, breaking my thoughts."

"I do!" I yelled, not paying attention to my Freudian slip.

Afterwards, we washed off and stepped out the shower. Walking back in the room, I noticed my clothes were gone and there were two racks of clothes in the middle of the room. I looked through the racks to see dresses, pants, skirts, tops, and jackets from Prada, Dior, and Dolce & Gabbana. There were also shoes from the top designers. I had died and gone to heaven. I picked out a cute Dior outfit, and went with a pair of Jimmy Choo stilettos. There were tons of panties and bras along with hosiery. I was in love.

Kenneth came from the bathroom. "Pick out what you like and the rest can go back."

I gave my infamous pout. I loved it all. "What if I want it all?" I tried to say like I was joking, knowing full well I wasn't.

"Then, you shall have it all." I went to get my makeup box, and noticed it wasn't mine. It was full of makeup, a different box, and different makeup. I looked over at Kenneth. "Out with the old, in with the new," he simply said.

He was top notch. I happily skipped back to the bathroom and got ready for my knight in shining armor. When I came out, I did a fashion model turn for him and his smile showed he approved. I saw the clothes had already been packed and Kenneth was dressed, so all we had to do was leave.

We went to the airport and I learned he had a private jet. I didn't know why he hadn't had a girlfriend or wife already, but there was no way I was letting him slip through my fingers. We partied in Vegas without a care in the world. We ate at fancy restaurants and played on the high roller tables. On the fifth night in Vegas, Kenneth presented me with a five carat, princess cut diamond ring with the band adorned in diamonds. I said yes before he could even get the question out. He said he didn't want to wait any longer and wanted to marry me right then. He promised we could take our time to have a big bang wedding, and I was ready to have access to all he had immediately, so I agreed. I was with my fairytale man and was going to have my fairytale wedding to live my fairytale life. I couldn't ask for more.

Careful What You Wish For

I had it. Everything I had ever wished for had come true. I was married to a rich and fine young man. I lived in a big, beautiful mansion. We had two maids, a gardener, a cook, and a live in nanny. I must have gotten pregnant that first time we had sex because that next month, I found out I was pregnant. But, that wasn't a problem. As I said before, guaranteed child support. We planned to have platinum wedding after I had the baby and dropped the baby weight.

I found it odd that the housekeepers did all the shopping and made sure my closet stayed with new stuff, but I didn't question it because morning sickness had taken its toll on me. When I finally started feeling better, I was so tired I didn't care to do anything. I just knew I'd be jet setting with Kenneth on his different speaking engagements and enjoying the fab life, but I was pregnant and had no energy for anything.

Once I had Jordyn though, I was ready to stake my claim as Kenneth's wife and let my position be known to anyone around. He took me to a few dinner parties and events, but he seemed so bored with me. I couldn't remember him introducing me as his wife, I felt more of an accessory. Afraid that I had gained weight with the pregnancy, I worked out twice as heard and barely ate anything. Kenneth wouldn't look at me, would barely touch me. I was being punished, but for what?

"You know I wanted a son," he finally said one day.

"Too bad we couldn't put in a special order in with the gender gods," I joked.

Kenneth jumped up and slapped me. "You think this shit is funny? You have to do one thing, bitch, and you fuck that up."

I held my cheek in disbelief. I couldn't believe that nigga just hit me. Fuck all the money he had, that shit wasn't worth it. "You know what, nigga, fuck you," I spat.

"Fuck me, huh?" He punched me in the chest between my breasts, he got close to me, and then started sucking my nipples.

Tears fell down my face. "Get off me," I whimpered.

He shook his head. "You belong to me now, Jennifer. I was going to tear this prenup up, but you fucked up and had a girl. I suggest you read this carefully, because starting tomorrow, everything needs to be done exactly how it's written out." He laughed and left the house.

I was confused. What the hell was he talking about? When he gave me that ring and I knew his worth, I didn't care what the prenup said. I figured it was some shit about me not cheating and not trying to take all his money or some shit like that. I took a seat at the kitchen table and read all twenty five pages, word for word.

Silly of me, when I signed that prenup, I agreed to not have access to anything, the reasoning why the housekeepers did all the shopping for my things. I even agreed that if we bore children and we divorced, custody would go to Kenneth and he would never pay me anything. Also, everything that I had before him, I had to give it up. Clothes, Taliary, car, shoes; everything. He didn't want me wearing things that another man had bought for me. My closet was full of designer names and my home was gorgeous, so I didn't mind losing old shit. Long as he replaced my stuff with better stuff, who was I to complain? I even agreed to be his trophy wife. I had to be picture perfect twenty four seven. We had cooks, but I was to cook his meals and serve him. I was never to look him directly in the eyes and I could never raise my voice. If I went to social gatherings with him, I was there to look pretty and nothing else. I wasn't allowed to socialize with anyone else and I was to never be out of his eyesight. If I left the house, I had to be escorted by a bodyguard, but there was no reason for me to leave because we had someone that would run any errands that needed to be ran. The nanny would take Jordyn to all doctor appointments. I never thought to read it in full because it was too long and I figured it was just full of some legal mumbo jumbo that wasn't even interesting. Rushing toward being a trophy wife, I signed up to be a personal slave. That was bullshit, and I wasn't going for it.

Once Kenneth arrived home, I threw the prenup in his face and told him I'd leave before I agreed to any of that bullshit. He gave me a sinister smirk. "But, you already agreed, babe." He looked as if he were pondering the situation. "You know what, go ahead and leave. Go back to nothing. What, are you going to do, ho your way back into an apartment and another car? You're a useless piece of trash. Do you think I didn't check you out before we got married? I know you were bed hopping with any nigga with money, hoping to cash out. You have nothing. I overlooked it because, damn, you can work that mouth and you're fine, but you're a dime a dozen. Maybe you didn't read the most important part of the prenup. If you try to leave, you will have to work off your debt."

"What muthafuckin' debt? I ain't bought shit. I been pregnant this whole time."

"Where do you think the clothes and shoes came from? Who do you think pays for the maids to take care of you and Jordyn? Who do you think I was paying to fuck me while your lazy ass was too sick and sleepy? While you're thinking about what you want to do, come over here and suck my dick."

"Suck your own dick." He knew I was from the hood, and I ain't give a shit about that money power bullshit he was on.

He shook his head again. "Did you not read the part about not raising your voice to me? I'm going to ask again nicely, and if you don't obey, I will be forced to use a different tactic."

"Fuck you, Kenneth. You still that nerdy lil' nigga everybody capped on in school. Just 'cause you got a few dollars don't mean shit. I dogged you in school and you still was beggin' for this pussy." His eyes went dark and I got scared, but I wouldn't show it. There was no way Kenneth would really hurt me. I was thinking he wanted to flaunt his money and power since he was the nerd everybody fucked with and now he was every woman's dream. He was on something much deeper.

He walked up to me and grabbed me by my throat. He lifted me off the ground as I tried to pry his fingers loose. "You will do as I say," he paused, "or you will die." His grip became tighter and tears welled up in my eyes. "Now, get the fuck down on your knees and suck my dick like you did that first time in the room. If you disobey me, I will fucking kill you, bitch," he said between clenched teeth.

My heart was racing. Could he really kill? Would he really kill me? The look in his eyes told me he would. Not wanting to chance it, I fought for air as I tried to shake my head yes in agreement. He let me go and I slid down to my knees and began to unbutton and unzip his pants. Tears flowed down my face as I sucked him exactly like I did the first time. Even with smelling another woman on him, I didn't dare say anything. He did as before, and grabbed handfuls of hair, but that time, he pulled harder and was rougher with me. He fucked my face so hard I thought he was trying to poke his dick through the back of my neck. I tried with all my might to suck him real good so that he would cum fast. My jaws began to get tired and I wanted to stop. I looked up at him and his eyes were closed as he pumped my face furiously. *Please, let this nightmare end*, I prayed. Finally, he exploded in my mouth and pushed me to the floor.

"Get pretty before you get in the bed, and be up by four thirty in the morning to have my breakfast ready."

Kenneth turned and walked out the kitchen, and I sat on the floor and cried. What had I gotten myself into?

The last eight months of my life had been a living nightmare. I was a shell of myself, walking around in a haze all the time. I felt like a Stepford wife. I had a strict schedule I had to keep to, whether Kenneth was home or not. There were cameras all around the house, so I didn't even have privacy to piss by myself. I got up at the crack of dawn every single day, got pretty, and made breakfast. I had to make lunch, too, because sometimes Kenneth would come home, sometimes he wouldn't, but he always watched that camera to see if I did as told. I had to clean the house from top to bottom. Why the fuck did we even have maids? I hated Kenneth, and I hated myself for being so blinded by money.

No matter what, Kenneth was always home by six, and he always wanted me to look like I was ready to go on a photoshoot with dinner on the table. He'd always take a bite or two and toss the rest to the side. There were times I wanted to kill myself, but I thought about Jordyn. Who would she have in her corner? Kenneth never paid attention to her, I didn't even think she knew he was her daddy. I had to get away, but how? Everybody watched me like hawks. They knew he would beat me, but nobody did anything. When he got mad enough to punch me in the face and I had a black eye or busted lip, he made me stay in and extra room until I was 'pretty' again.

I undressed and got in the shower. Soon as I poured the peach soap on my sponge, I wanted to throw up. I hated the smell of peaches, but it had intoxicated him so that first time and he knew I used it to lure his senses, that he required that to be the only smell on me.

I put on a Dior dress, combed down my wrap, and applied my makeup. There was a time I would die to play dress up and just sit around and look pretty. Now, I hated it. I wanted to rip that dress to shreds and toss all the makeup in the garbage.

Broken

Jordyn had just turned a year old. There was nothing special. No big party filled with fabulous decorations or gifts. Kenneth didn't even acknowledge her. I felt like shit. I went through my normal day and managed to bake her a cupcake. I hoped Kenneth didn't get upset. I almost held my breath when I heard him come through the front door. I didn't care to breathe another designer name, but I had on some high price label. I greeted him with a smile and saw he had a woman on his arms. I almost frowned, but quickly hid it, smiled at her, and said hello.

"Oh, baby, she's a doll. I want her right now."

Kenneth turned to the high fashion wannabe and kissed her. He groped her shamelessly as I stood there and watched. He hadn't touched me in months. I had sucked plenty of dick and swallowed plenty of cum, but that was the extent of sexual contact for me. I knew the tears were in my eyes, but I dared them to drop.

"Misa, Kimberly wants you."

I choked back a cough. "What?"

She boldly stepped to me and kissed me on my mouth, then put her arms around me and stuck her tongue in my mouth. I was baffled. Before I could react one way or another, Kenneth put his arms around both of us. He put his hand through my hair gently and almost lovingly.

"Give her whatever she wants, Misa," he whispered.

He rubbed my body and I felt a spark of sexual energy shoot up my spine. I needed the physical connection. With tears falling down my face, I allowed her tongue to roam my mouth. Kenneth kissed Kimberly's neck as he put my hand on his dick. I stroked him as I watched him lust for another woman. Before I knew it, Kenneth and Kimberly were kissing. Kenneth pushed my head down, letting me know he wanted his dick sucked. I quietly got on her knees, freed his hardness, and did my job. So many thought ran through my mind. I had no idea what was about to happen. I was at her breaking point and couldn't take it any longer. I abruptly stopped sucking Kenneth's dick when I heard him moaning and whispering sweet nothings to Kimberly.

"I can't do this, Kenneth," I whispered as I stood up.

"Babe, go to the room," he told Kimberly.

"I'm so hot and horny. Please hurry. I want her so bad." Kimberly pinched my nipple before she walked off.

Once she was safely upstairs, Kenneth slapped me so hard, I stumbled backwards. "Bitch, are you crazy? I own you, and you will do what the fuck I want."

"I'm not into women, Kenneth. You can't make me do this." I felt she had to stand up for something. Maybe that would make Kenneth respect me.

Kenneth smiled and then held me against the wall by my neck. That seemed to be his favorite way to restrain me. "Not into women? Hmm, what were you into when you and Sally," my eyes got big, "had a little romp with the senator?" I wondered how he knew about that as Kenneth kicked opened my legs to spread them apart. "Or, what were you into when you and Tina would let men pay you to watch both of you munch carpet until you passed out?" He lightly rubbed my hardened clit. As much as I didn't want to be turned on, I was. I wasn't a lesbian, but I did like playing with women every once in a while. "Listen and listen good. I like Kimberly, and apparently, she likes you. If you disappoint her, my wrath will not be pretty." He stopped rubbing my clit when he felt me trying to grind on his hand. I wanted to cum so bad. He licked his fingers. "I forgot how wet and sweet this pussy was. I may have to start fucking you more often. Now, go upstairs and be a good girl for me," he whispered in my ear.

I had been at the verge of an orgasm when Kenneth stopped stroking my starving clit. I wanted to scream, but I sucked it up. How bad could it be? It wasn't like I would be doing something I hadn't done before. I figured I could get sexually pleased, and maybe do something good for my husband and make him love me again. I put on a smile for him. "Yes, baby.

Once we got upstairs, Kimberly had already undressed herself and was lying across the bed playing with herself.

"You started without us," Kenneth said as he undressed. "Make her cum." he ordered me.

I dropped my dress as I walked over to the bed. I positioned herself between Kimberly's legs and skillfully licked her clit. "Oh my, this feels delightful," Kimberly purred. I lifted her legs and licked every inch of Kimberly that I could. I didn't want to admit it, but Kimberly tasted good. I was dripping wet, and I couldn't wait to feel Kimberly's mouth on me, or feel my husband inside of me. I planned to lick Kimberly's pussy better than it had ever been licked to make her happy like Kenneth wanted me to. "Yes, yes!" Kimberly screamed out. She grabbed my hair and held my face between her legs. "Right there, baby. Yes, baby. Oh your pretty ass is going to make me cum!" Once Kimberly shook and came, Kenneth grabbed my hair and turned me toward him so I could suck his dick.

"That's right, get it nice and hard, baby."

Kimberly got on her knees behind me and pinched my nipples as she kissed my back. I let out a moan because it felt so good. She began rubbing on my clit, moaning as I sucked Kenneth's dick. Just as I was about to cum, Kimberly stopped rubbing my clit. They were torturing me and I felt like they knew it. If I had just had one release, I would be OK.

"I need to feel that hot pussy," Kenneth said.

Finally, I thought. I got up and felt butterflies as I thought of feeling Kenneth inside of me. As I was about to straddle him, he pushed me to the side.

He laid Kimberly on her stomach and entered her from behind. I was lost as she watched my husband fill up some strange woman. She moaned and purred, and I knew it felt good to Kimberly.

"Lay in front of me, baby," Kimberly said to me.

I did as told. I figured at least I would finally be able to cum. Instead, I was so disappointed. Kimberly would lick my clit once, then did a lot of moaning, concentrating more on Kenneth's deep strokes. She came, and I felt like she was more turned on by me being there watching them. She knew she was fucking my husband in my face. Finally, Kenneth picked Kimberly up, turned her over, and fucked her missionary as he kissed her passionately. He came inside of Kimberly and then looked up at me.

"Your makeup is fucked up. Go get yourself together," he said evenly.

"Yea, baby, get ready for round two," Kimberly said.

I felt used and humiliated. I hated Kenneth and Kimberly, and wanted to kill them both. I looked over at Kimberly as I walked to the bathroom. She looked just like I did a couple of years ago. She was fresh and vibrant, and she looked like she was trying to set her trap to be a trophy wife.

Breaking Free

It had been two months since Kimberly first came over. After that first day, she was over often. I had been moved to another room and she was in my bed. Sometimes I had to watch, sometimes they wanted privacy, but I could still hear them. I didn't know what I was going to do. I was a prisoner. I had no one to call and no one to help. No one cared about me. I could disappear and no one would notice. I woke up one morning for my daily routine and accidentally walked in on Kenneth and Kimberly having sex. My interruption was right before Kenneth was about to cum and I pissed him off. He punched me, made me suck his dick to get him back hard, and then sent me away as he continued to fuck Kimberly. How couldn't she see that he would do the same to her? I had to get away.

One of the maids, Sonja, was going out for household stuff. I knew she would take the minivan because she had to also take Jordyn to the doctor. After Kenneth left for work, I slipped out the house and hid in the back of the van. I was so small, I used some stuff that was already back there and put it over me. I hoped Sonja didn't want to look in the back before the doctor visit. I felt so relieved that the doctor was at a hospital. The garage was full of cars, and I was able to get out after Sonja and Jordyn were inside.

I had no idea what my plan was going to be, but I had to do something. *Think, think.* I was actually home free. I could have left and been away, but I couldn't leave Jordyn. I loved her and I couldn't leave her with heartless ass Kenneth.

After finding where Sonja was with Jordyn, I kept my distance and watched. They were called to the back, and I saw them walk in a room. The doctors and nurses were walking about, so I decided to be bold.

"Look, Sonja, you know how it is. I just want my baby."

"Mama," Jordyn said.

"How did you get here?" Sonja whispered as if Kenneth would hear them.

"Please. Just let me take my baby and leave."

I wondered what was going through Sonja's mind at that time. She looked like a million thoughts ran through her mind. Finally, she said, "Here's sixty. You better get away fast and go as far as you can."

I didn't give it a second thought. I snatched up Jordyn and left out of the hospital as quick as I could. It seemed to be a miracle that the bus station was about a block away from the hospital. I purchased a ticket to get on the next bus that was pulling out in about ten minutes. Before boarding, I bought a few snacks and a small pack of diapers.

As I sat in the back, I wondered what the hell I was going to do. I had ten dollars. I didn't have anyone to call and nowhere to go. I was on the bus for a day before it reached some small town. I got off and went inside the station. I stretched for a while, then found myself sleep in a chair. When I woke up to a crying Jordyn, I found out I had missed my bus. My stomach was growling, so I figured I'd find somewhere and get a bag of chips or something to hold me over and get Jordyn some more milk. As I walked down the street, I knew I looked a mess. My hair hadn't been combed, I had on the same clothes from the day before, and my makeup was a mess.

Feeling defeated, I sat down on a bench and cried. A car pulled up and the lady driving asked me if I needed help. I sniffled and wiped my face. "No, thank you. I'm fine."

"You're not fine. At the least, let me offer you a hot meal and some clothes to change into."

I looked at the elderly woman. It could have been a trick. Kenneth could have sent someone after me. "I'm on the way home now. Thank you."

The woman got out the car. "Don't be afraid. I just want to help. You need some food, she needs some food."

"You don't know anything about me," I said defensively.

"I know the bruises. I can see the remainders of a black eye. I can see the swollen lip. Please, let me give you a safe place to go. No matter how much he says he will stop, he won't."

I started crying. "I know." I whispered.

The woman gave me a hug. "It's OK. You're OK now."

She walked me to her car and took me to her home. On the ride, I whispered, "Kenneth is a wealthy and powerful man. He will find me."

"Don't worry. Ms. Agnes will take care of everything."

Over the next few days, I purged my soul and told Ms. Agnes everything, even my real name. I no longer wanted to be that platinum digging, trophy wife Misa. I simply wanted to be Jennifer Freeman, the round the way girl from the Bay Area. Not long after that. Ms. Agnes gave me my her divorce papers that had the agreement I could have full custody of Jordyn and Kenneth wouldn't pay anything in child support. I gladly accepted, feeling blessed to get out alive and with my daughter. I never knew how Ms. Agnes did it, but I was grateful, and never took for granted the precious moments of life, and being able to make my own way.

I enrolled in school and got a job at a local motel cleaning rooms. I never thought I'd do anything like that, but was grateful for the second chance to really live my life and enjoy a hard day's work.

Lost And Found
Keontay Vaughn

<u>Chapter 1</u>

Amber stood over the sink staring in the mirror at her busted lip and steadily swelling eye. She had to be to work in a little over an hour and there was absolutely no way for her to conceal her latest fight with Jason. She had considered not going in, but it would be her third time calling out that week. She wasn't sure she'd have a job at the end of the week if she called out again. As she stood trying to contemplate what to do, she was snapped out of her thoughts by the sound of Jason trying to come in the bathroom.

"Amber, open the door." He wiggled the knob. "Baby, I'm sorry. Please, just open the door."

"Jason, you're high and drunk, and I don't wanna fight with you anymore." Amber backed away from the door as a precaution.

"Please, baby. I promise I won't hit you again. I just need to see your face," Jason pleaded.

Reluctantly, Amber opened the door and Jason was standing there with a look of remorse on his face, but it wasn't a face she hadn't seen before. When he reached out to touch her face, she flinched.

"Baby, I'm really sorry." Jason pulled her over to him. "You forgive me?"

"Mmmhmm." Amber kept her eyes on the floor.

"I love you." Jason started kissing her neck, cheek, and eventually made his way to her lips. "You love me?"

"Yea," Amber mumbled.

"Say it." Jason started to undo Amber's shirt. "Tell me you love me."

"I---love---you," Amber said with slight hesitation.

Jason laid Amber back on the bed and proceeded to *make love* to her. As soon as it was over, he rolled over and went to sleep. Amber went back into the bathroom and showered. As hard as she tried, she couldn't fight the tears that ran down her cheeks. After she got out of the shower, she stood in the mirror and took time to apply makeup to her bruised eye, and applied an ice pack back on her lip hoping to relieve some of the swelling before she got to work. She grabbed her purse and keys, and placed them by the door. Right on time, her best friend, Danielle, was at the door ringing the doorbell. She went into her daughter Ariel's room and grabbed the sleeping baby girl, threw on her sunglasses, and headed out the door.

"What the hell happened to your face, Amber?" Danielle asked, pulling the sunglasses off Amber's face.

"D, it's nothing." Amber handed Ariel to Danielle. "I have to get going. I can't be late again," she said as she put her sunglasses back on.

"You know what..." Danielle started.

"Not now, Danielle. I love you and I'll see you later." Amber hugged her best friend and kissed her daughter, and then got in her car.

When Amber arrived at work, there was a note on her computer for her to report to her supervisor's office immediately upon her arrival. After sitting down her purse at her desk, she went into Mr. Grant's office.

"Mr. Grant, you wanted to see me?" Amber cautiously entered.

"Have a seat, Ms. Anderson, and would you mind removing those sunglasses. You are in the building after all," Mr. Grant stated without bothering to look up from the files he was reviewing.

"Is there a problem, Mr. Grant?" Amber removed her sunglasses, but kept her head down.

"Well, Ms. Anderson, it appears that your performance the last few weeks has dropped significantly, and more importantly, you're attendance has been less than stellar. As a result, everyone else has been picking up your slack."

"Mr. Grant, I apologize for my attendance and my performance, but I can assure you that it won't happen again and things will be..."

"Ms. Anderson, I'm sorry, but we're going to have to let you go. It appears that your personal life is having a major affect on your professional life. If you were my daughter, the man whom you're involved with would be a dead man right about now." Mr. Grant came to Amber's side. "I can't tell you what to do, Ms. Anderson, but for the sake of you and your daughter, you might need to reconsider your relationship. Here's a number that might help you if and when you're ready." He handed her a card with some information written on it.

Amber went back to her desk, packed up her things, and left work. She knew that going home would start a fight, so she headed over to Danielle's house, knowing full well she'd have to explain what happen between her and Jason earlier that morning. When she got to Danielle's, she wiped the tears she'd cried on the way over and used her key to get in. Ariel saw her before Danielle did.

"Mama." Ariel walked unsteadily with arms outstretched toward her mother.

"Hey, munchkin." Amber picked up her daughter and kissed her over and over again.

"Amber, what are you doing here?" Danielle asked, glancing at the clock on the wall.

"I got fired today." Amber sighed. "I don't know what the hell I'ma do now."

"How in the...what did you get fired for?"

"Mr. Grant said my work performance has been on the decline and my attendance has been kinda bad lately."

"And, why is that?" Danielle asked matter of factly.

"I've just been dealing with a lot lately. You know, weaning Ariel off the pacifier and what not, then just haven't been sleeping well."

"And, what's going on with Jason?" Danielle prodded a little more.

"Nothing."

"C'mon now, you really gonna come at me like that, baby girl?" Danielle pulled the sunglasses off Amber's face. "You gon' tell me that this black eye and that busted lip is a result of nothing?"

Amber's tears started falling. She put Ariel down on the floor and went over to the bay window in Danielle's living room. "D, I love him so much. I just can't walk away from him now. We've been through too much together. If I turn my back on him now, only God knows what's gonna happen. Ariel needs her dad."

"Amber, I know you think you love him, but this ain't love. Late nights in the ER, covering bruises with makeup, hiding black eyes behind shades, none of that is good. Ariel needs a real man in her life. Do you want her to grow up thinking that it is okay to let some dude put his hands on her? It's not just you anymore. You have a daughter to think about. If you don't leave Jason for any other reason, you need to leave him for her."

"Danielle, you just don't understand. Do you mind keeping Ariel for a little while longer so I can go handle some business?"

"Sure, I'll see you this afternoon."

"Thanks."

Amber said goodbye to her best friend, kissed her daughter, and then headed back to her car. She drove around for an hour or so trying to figure out how she would break the news to Jason. Somehow, she knew he was going to turn the whole situation around on her. All she could do was pray that he was sober when she talked to him and that it didn't turn into some big blow up. After debating on when and how to tell him, she just decided to go home and talk to him. Upon arriving at their townhouse she didn't see his car in the parking lot, so she headed inside to wait for him.

Amber started cleaning the house from the remnants of their fight earlier that morning. There was broken glass left on the kitchen floor leading into the living room. She vacuumed up the dirt that was scattered across the floor from the plant that got knocked over. Once everything was cleaned up, she started some lunch. She figured it was the least she could do since she was already home. Every time she heard a car near her house, she got extremely nervous, her palms started to sweat, and her heart pounded like a bass drum.

"Amber!" Jason walked in the house slamming the door so hard that pictures of their family fell from the wall.

"I'm i-i-in here," Amber answered nervously.

"Where the hell you been?" Jason stormed into the kitchen.

"Whatchu mean?" Amber sat his plate of food on the table.

"Amber, right now is really not a good time for you to start this shit with me," he said, knocking the plate of food off the table. "I went to your job and they told me you got fired and left as soon as you got there this morning, so where the hell have you been since then?"

"I went to Danielle's to check on Ariel and then I came straight home. I swear." Amber backed away from Jason.

"What the hell did you do to get fired?" he asked, grabbing Amber by the collar.

"Jason, it wasn't my fault. I swear. He...they said my attendance lately was too bad and..." Amber attempted to get free from Jason's grip.

"So, whose fault was it? Huh, Amber?" Jason threw her down to the floor.

"Jason, please. You promised," Amber backed herself into the corner and drew her knees to her chest.

"Get up." Jason grabbed her by the arm and pulled her to her feet. "Are you trying to say this was my fault? Huh? I don't hear you talking, Amber!"

"No, that's not what I meant, I just..." Amber stumbled over her words.

"You just what?"

"I couldn't go to work when you...I mean when we..."

Before she could finish her statement, she saw Jason's fist coming at her. Try as she might, Amber couldn't block the blow that was coming toward her. The first hit made her legs give out and no sooner than she hit the floor, the second blow was Jason's steel toe boot, crashing her rib cage so hard she could have sworn she felt it shatter.

"J-J-Jason please, I-I-I I'm sorry." Amber curled herself up into the fetal position.

"Clean this mess up and don't leave this damn house!"

Jason left Amber laying there in a puddle of her own tears and blood. Once she gathered the strength to get up, she called Danielle to ask if Ariel could spend the night with her. After assuring Danielle that she was fine, she started to clean the kitchen. After the kitchen was cleaned, she went to her and Jason's bedroom and took a hot shower, took some pain killers, and then got into bed. She was almost certain that Jason had broken her ribs, but she knew another visit to the hospital was out of the question. Not to mention, she didn't want to risk making Jason angrier by leaving the house after he told her not to.

Chapter 2

Amber hoped and prayed that by the time he came back home that he wasn't angry and that he hadn't been drinking or smoking again. When Jason finally crept back into the house around four a.m., in his hands he held a bouquet of roses, a teddy bear, and a small, square box.

"Baby, you sleep?" Jason brushed the hair back away from her face.

"No." Amber blinked back the tears that were in welling up in her eyes.

"I'm sorry, baby girl." He laid the teddy bear next to her. "I love you." He took a ring out of the box he'd brought in with him. "I wanna make you my wife." Jason slid the ring on her finger. "I promise that things are going to get better. Okay?"

"Okay," Amber replied in a whisper.

Jason got in the bed. Amber cringed as he pulled her into his arms. Tears came rushing from her eyes as if someone had cracked a dam. She forced her face into the pillow to muffle the sounds of her sobs. She laid there with only her tears to comfort her. As soon as she was sure Jason was asleep, she slipped out of bed and went into the restroom. When Amber closed the bathroom door, she removed her gown and stood staring at her black and blue torso. Just lifting her arm sent pains shooting through her chest and rib cage.

"Jason?" Amber gently shook him.

"What, Amber? It's early as hell." Jason rolled over and covered his head with the pillow.

"I think I need to go to the ER."

"For what?" Jason threw off the covers and sat straight up in bed.

"I, uh, I think maybe my ribs are broke."

"Damn man." Jason started dressing. "What hospital?"

"County." Amber wrapped her robe around herself.

"You ain't gonna put no clothes on?" Jason froze in his tracks and stared at Amber.

"It hurts to move too much." Amber hoped her answer would appease him.

"So what! I mean, you need to me help you or something?"

"No." Amber slowly and meticulously unwrapped her robe and began putting on her clothes.

"Yo, I'll be in the car."

Jason left out, slamming the door behind him as Amber continued dressing through her tears. She moved as fast as her pain would allow her. She could hear Jason in front of the house practically laying on the horn. As soon as she prepared to walk out the door, Jason was heading back in on a war path.

"What the hell you wake me up for if you weren't ready?" Jason yelled as they walked to the car.

"I was ready but you…" Amber stopped herself. "I'm sorry it took so long, it just hurts really badly."

"Yea, whatever, just get in the car."

The ride to the hospital was filled with so much tension, Amber almost felt like it was hard for her to breathe. Jason dropped her off at the front entrance, and then went to park the car. By the time Amber checked herself in, she realized she actually was having difficulty breathing. The nurse escorted her to the back and got her set up on some oxygen while the waited for the doctor. After her oxygen levels were up to par and stable, the doctor came in to see Amber by this time Jason had made his way back to the room.

"So, Ms. Anderson, what brings you into the emergency room this morning?"

"She tripped over one of our baby girl's toys and took a tumble down the stairs," Jason spoke up before Amber could. "We thought she was fine, but she's got some pretty rough looking bruises and she was complaining about being really sore on her right side of her chest, so we were thinking maybe she broke something. Right, babe?" Jason gently stroked Amber's face.

Amber said nothing. She just shook her head in agreement and gave a reassuring smile. The doctor continued to take notes while stealing glances at the non-verbal communication going on between Amber and Jason. He sensed there was more to the story, but he knew he wouldn't get anything as long as Jason and Amber were together.

"Mr. Anderson?"

"No," Jason answered, "its Mr. Stephenson. Amber's my fiancée."

"Oh okay. Mr. Stephenson, we're gonna take Ms. Anderson to get some x-rays, so just hang tight here for me and we'll get her back ASAP."

"Okay," Jason kissed Amber on her forehead. "Love you. See you in a few."

The nurse helped Amber into a wheel chair as the doctor scribbled a few more notes hurriedly onto her chart. Once Amber was settled, the nurse grabbed the chart, read over the notes, and wheeled Amber out of the room. As soon as she was sure they were out of ear shot, the questions began.

"So, Ms. Anderson, how long have you been engaged?"

"A few days, but we've been together six years and we have a two year old little girl."

"Aww, I bet she's adorable."

"Yea." Amber smiled. "She's the reason I get up every day."

"Has it always been this bad?"

"Huh?" Amber was thrown for a loop by the question.

"Black eye, busted lips, possible broken ribs. I'm a medical professional, so I can tell what comes from a fall down some steps and what comes from an abusive relationship."

"It's the first time..."

"No, more like the third time in the last several months. I pulled your charts. Sprain wrist two months ago, broken nose a month before that, and broken ankle six and a half months ago. Just because you might go from hospital to hospital doesn't mean your records disappear."

The nurse helped Amber up onto the table and positioned her so that she could get the best possible x-rays in the least amount of shots. Upon finishing them, she sat down with Amber as they wait for the films.

"Look, Ms. Anderson, I can't tell you what to do, but I can say this, you have a daughter. Do you want this to be her life when she gets older? Hospital visits? Lying about make believe accidents? I'm a survivor of domestic violence and I've gone through it myself, no matter how many promises he makes, if he hasn't changed by now, baby girl, he's not gonna change."

Amber was at a loss for words as she made no attempts to wipe the tears that were cascading down her cheeks. The nurse handed her some tissue and got her films from the x-ray technician, and then they headed back to her room to wait for the doctor to exam the films. As they rounded the corner to her room, they could see Jason pacing the halls.

"Dang, what took y'all so long?" Jason questioned once Amber was settled back in the bed.

"We had to take our time as to not prevent more injury to Ms. Anderson's ribs, chest, or lungs."

"Nurse, is there any way I can get something for the pain?"

"Let me double check with the doctor, then I'll be right back with you. Buzz me if you need anything in the mean time."

"Thanks." Amber tried to get as comfortable as possible in the bed.

"So, do they know if anything is broken yet?" Jason rested on the foot of the bed and nonchalantly flipped through channels on the TV.

"We've gotta wait for the doctor to review the films and see what's what."

"Oh." Jason glanced at his watch for the third time since Amber had come back to the room. "I gotta go meet up with some peeps at the studio, I texted Danielle to let her know you was here, so I'm sure she'll be here soon." Jason's lips barely grazed Ambers before he disappeared out the door.

Amber was actually relieved that Jason was gone, but she hated being at the hospital alone. Moments after Jason left, the nurse returned with the doctor and some pain medication. He confirmed that two of her ribs were indeed fractured and it would take about six weeks for them to heal. The doctor instructed Amber to ice the injury at least two to three times daily and get as much rest as possible. As the doctor was preparing her discharge paperwork, Danielle arrived.

"Two broken ribs, Amber?" Danielle stared at Amber in utter disbelief.

"It's nothing, D, I just wanna get some meds and lay down, please."

Danielle silently helped her best friend into the car and then got behind the wheel. Neither woman had much of anything to say. Through the faint hints of the coming of dawn and the splashes of the dulling street lights that entered the car, both Danielle and Amber's faces had remnants of the silent tears they shared. After stopping by the pharmacy, they went back to Danielle's house where Amber locked herself in the spare bedroom and cried herself to sleep.

Amber stayed at Danielle's house locked in her spare bedroom for three weeks before Jason had grown tired of being ignored. Danielle had done a decent job of keeping Ariel occupied while trying to keep her friend from falling deeper and deeper into a dark depression, and keeping her from going back home to Jason.

"Hey, Amber," Danielle said after lightly tapping on the door, "I'm gonna go to the grocery store. You wanna tag along?"

Amber lay silently in the pitch black room, ignoring Danielle's attempts to get her out of the house. When she heard the door creaking open, she shut her eyes to the slither of light that broke the darkness and pretended to be fast asleep. Danielle sighed and closed the door back.

"Mama sleep?" Ariel's tiny voice questioned.

"Yea, mama's still sleeping," Danielle responded broken hearted.

Amber's tears flooded her eyes at the sound of both her daughter's voice, and at the pain and sadness in her best friends. She knew she had to get better and snap out of the darkness that was enveloping all around her. When Danielle and Ariel returned from the store, Amber was freshly showered and in the kitchen attempting to find something to cook for lunch.

"Mama!" Ariel wrapped her arms around Amber's leg. "Mama no sleepy no more."

"No, mommy's awake now." Amber smoothed Ariel's curly, frazzled hair.

"Good to see you up and about," Danielle mumbled while putting groceries away.

"D, thanks for everything you've done for me, for us." Amber hugged her best friend as if her life depended on it, ignoring the sharp pains shooting through her still sore ribcage. "I love you like a sister, you know that."

"Yea, I know." Danielle fought back tears. "I love you more."

"D, I've gotta go home, I have to deal with Jason and this whole."

"Amber, c'mon! I need you to be smart about this. Do you really think three weeks apart is gonna change anything?"

"I don't know Danielle, but I can't...I won't just walk away without trying."

"You can't walk away without trying? Really? So, what the hell have the past six and half years been if not you trying and him just getting progressively worse with his abuse! Is it gonna take him hurting her," Danielle looked over at Ariel playing contently in a corner, "for you to really get the picture that he's not gonna change and he doesn't give a good goddamn about you or her!"

"Danielle, you don't understand, you never will, you've never been in my shoes." Amber headed to the spare bedroom to start packing.

"Please, explain it to me." Danielle was hot on her heels. "I cannot and will not let you take my goddaughter into that malicious environment until you can give me just cause as to why you feel the need to take your ass back there. I mean, you do realize that your fractured ribs are still not healed? All you have to do is piss him off one good time and it'll take one blow for him to kill you! Do you even care about that at all? If you're gone, who's gonna be his next victim, Amber?"

"Danielle, please." Amber continued packing.

"Fine. It's your life. Don't call me the next time he goes upside your head." Danielle stormed out of the guestroom and into her bedroom.

Amber finished packing her and Ariel's things. Although she hated to leave things the way they were with Danielle, she knew there was no changing Danielle's mind about Jason or about her going back to him.

Amber figured three weeks was more than enough time for the two of them to have thought and processed things, but there was still a nervousness that caused her stomach to do flips as she neared their house. When they pulled up, Amber didn't see Jason's car or motorcycle parked out front. She went inside and fell almost instantly back into her old routine. She put Ariel in the living room in front of the TV and went into the kitchen to start dinner.

"Daddy!" Ariel took off in the direction of her father as soon as he was partially in the door.

"There's daddy's baby girl." Jason dropped everything, scooped up his daughter in his arms, and headed to the kitchen where Amber was. "I missed y'all."

"We missed you, too." Amber felt and heard a sense of sincerity in Jason's voice.

After dinner and a movie, Jason gave Ariel a bath and read her a bedtime story. While he was putting her to bed, Amber went and showered. By the time she got out, Jason was in their bedroom lying across their bed watching the news, but he turned off the TV when she came in the room.

"You aiight? I mean, you need anything?" Jason asked as he sat up.

"Nah, I'm good."

"I kinda thought you weren't gonna come back, that you were gonna take Ariel and run," Jason mentioned as Amber sat on the bed beside him.

"I'd be lying if I said I didn't contemplate it, but I need you to think about going to see a counselor if you really want us to be a family. We can't get married until that happens."

"Man, Amber, you know I'm not down with that counseling shit. I don't want people all up in my business."

"Not even if it means either saving or losing your family?" Amber voice was barely audible.

"So, what you saying? If I don't do this you're leaving? Try it and I bet you never see Ariel again. You forget you're the one without a job, and if we break up you got no place to live, so don't go making empty threats to me, Amber." Jason grabbed his helmet. "I'm going for a ride."

Jason left out and Amber thought about what he had said, so she resolved that first thing in the morning she was going to get back on the job hunt. She even contemplated moving out of her and Jason's place and getting a place of her own so that could never be held over her head again. She laid back in bed and prayed for guidance before drifting off to sleep.

Amber awoke the next morning to a note from Jason stating he and Ariel went to his parents' for the day. Amber got online and started her job search. She was absolutely tired of being tied to a desk in an office, so she decided to branch out. She found a couple of openings at the local Ys. After making a few calls, she decided to go fill out some applications and get her resume out there. One requirement for working in the childcare field was CPR certification. Being that she was free for the day, she decided to sign up for a class they were offering.

Chapter 3

While Amber was at the Y taking the CPR class, she ran into a woman named Chloe Daniels who owned a daycare. Mrs. Daniels offered Amber a job on a trial basis. She couldn't wait to share the good news with Danielle and Jason, thinking they'd both be over the moon happy for her. When she called Danielle, it went straight to voicemail so she left her a message. Pulling up to her house, she saw that Jason and Ariel were back.

"Babe?" she called as she walked in the front door.

"Shhh! I just got Ariel down." Jason jogged down the steps two at a time.

"I've got some great news." Amber dropped her purse and went into the kitchen.

"What?" Jason responded, seemingly uninterested.

"I've got a new job. I start next week."

"A job where? You didn't tell me you were getting another job already. What about Ariel? Who's gonna watch her?"

"It's at this daycare called Kid's Corner, Ariel will be able to go with me and I'll get an employee discount. I met the owner today while I was at the Y taking a CPR class and applying for some jobs."

"Why can't you just stay at home and take care of Ariel? I make more than enough to support us, and I ain't on that nine-to-five BS." Jason posted himself in the kitchen doorway.

"Jason, you already know I don't wanna be an at home mom. I stayed home with Ariel for three months instead of six weeks because you asked me to, but now she's old enough for daycare so…"

"You sure this ain't just a part of some plot for you to leave me?" Jason walked up behind Amber, who was now positioned between him and the stove."

"Jason, what are you talking about?" Amber's heart started racing as she felt Jason's six-foot, two hundred pound frame towering over her.

"Don't play dumb with me, Amber. You planning on leaving me since I won't go to counseling?" Jason turned Amber so they were face to face.

"No, Jason, I swear."

"Let me find out something different," Jason said before walking away.

Amber was beginning to think that maybe Danielle had been right and going back to Jason had been a bad idea. Then, she remember when she lost her job her boss had given her the card of someone who might be able to help her. After dinner was finished, Amber located the card and made a mental note to go check out the place on the card the next time she was alone. Unfortunately for her, since she told Jason about her new job he had been watching her like a hawk. Although they had yet to get into another physical altercation, Jason knew how and when to cut Amber to shreds with his words. On the bright side, however, Amber was settling into her new job nicely and Ariel loved being around the other kids at the daycare.

Amber nervously knocked on her boss' door. "Umm, Mrs. Daniels, can I talk to you for a second?"

"Sure, Amber, come in and have a seat." Chloe looked up from her computer. "What can I do for you?"

"I know I just started and all, but I was wonder if at all possible could I have a couple of hours off tomorrow. I know it is really last minute, but couple of weeks before I started here I had an, uh, an accident, and my follow up appointment is tomorrow. I forgot until today when they called and…"

"Amber," Chloe cut her off, "it's okay. Just let me know what time you'll be gone so I can make sure the desk is covered."

"My appointment is at ten. I should be back by lunch time." Amber let out a huge sigh of relief.

"Alrighty then, so we'll see you in around lunch."

Amber went back to work and the rest of the day flowed by without a hitch. After work, she called home and tried Jason on his cell to see what he wanted for dinner, but got no answer on either number, so she and Ariel decided to go to a little diner near the house and have dinner. She hadn't been to the diner in a while, but she loved it because it was small quite and homely. By the time they got home, Ariel was knocked out cold.

"Where you been?" Jason appeared out of the shadow of the hallway.

"Dammit, Jason, you scared me." Amber held Ariel tightly to her chest. "Why are you sitting in here in the dark?"

"I asked you a question." Jason followed Amber to Ariel's room.

"I took Ariel to the diner for some dinner." Amber laid Ariel on the bed, undressed her, put her PJs on, and then placed her in her bed. "I called you, but you didn't answer."

"Don't turn your back on me, Amber!" Jason whirled Amber around by her arm, causing her to lose her footing.

"Jason, what's wrong with you!" Amber slowly got up off the floor. "I wasn't turning my back on you. I was putting our daughter to bed. Have you been drinking or something?" Amber massaged the area of her arm where he'd grabbed her.

"So what if I have? We need to talk!" Jason reached for her again.

"Maybe a little bit later once you're sobered up." Amber moved out of his reach.

"Who do you think you're talking to?" Jason backhanded Amber, causing her to stumble, but not fall. Before Amber could regained her bearings, Jason had her pinned against the wall.

"Daddy?" Ariel sat up in her bed rubbing her eyes. "Mommy?"

"So, you gonna hit me in front of our daughter?" Amber asked with tear filled eyes.

Jason looked over at his baby girl staring up at him with a look of confusion upon her face, back to Amber, and then walked out. Amber sat on the foot of Ariel's bed. Try as she might, she couldn't hold back her tears any longer as they broke free and started to fall from her eyes.

"Mommy k?" Ariel nestled her way into Amber's lap.

"Yea, baby girl, mommy's okay." Amber wrapped her arms tightly around her daughter.

"Mommy sleep here?" Ariel looked up at her with pleading eyes.

"Okay."

Amber laid down on the bed next to Ariel and watched as she started drifting back to sleep. Lying there with her daughter, Amber realized she had finally reached her breaking point and it was time she started to put some sort of plan into action.

The next morning after showering and giving Ariel a bath, they left for the day. Once Amber dropped Ariel off at Kids Corner, she headed into the hospital for her follow up. When she got there, the nurse she saw the night she was in the emergency room was on duty.

"Ms. Anderson, what are you doing?" The nurse noticed the slight swelling on Amber's face. "Come with me."

"I just came for my follow up." Amber followed the nurse to the back.

"Hmmm okay." The nurse handed Amber an ice pack for her face. "Any new pain or swelling?"

"No, deep breathing still a little painful, but other than that I'm good as new."

"And that?" She pointed to Amber's face.

"The straw that broke the camel's back."

"That's good to hear. Do you have friends or family you can stay with?"

"It's a work in progress," Amber admitted.

After being cleared with the doctor, Amber headed to see the lady, Ms. Agnes that Mr. Grant had given her the information on. Amber walked down the block looking for the address written on the card, but Mr. Grant's hand writing was a bit difficult to decipher. In her attempts to read and walk, Amber bumped into an older woman who was carrying some groceries into her home and knocked the bag out of her hand.

"Oh my goodness, I'm so sorry." Amber quickly placed her sunglasses back on and helped the woman pick up her groceries. "I wasn't paying attention to where I was going."

"It's fine, young lady. No harm, no foul. Are you okay?" She took notice of the swelling on Amber's face and her darkened eye before she'd been so quick to slide her sunglasses on.

"Yes, ma'am."

"Why don't you come on in and have a glass of tea."

"Thank you, Ms...?"

"Agnes, everyone round here calls me Ms. Agnes."

"Really?" Tears instantly filled Amber's eyes.

"Child, you alright?" Ms. Agnes asked with concern in her voice.

"My old boss, Mr. Grant, sent me to come see you. He said you might be able to help me."

"Well, now you definitely need to come in and have some tea so we can talk."

Amber helped Ms. Agnes bring in the remainder of the groceries, and then they sat down with some tea. Amber gave Ms. Agnes the rundown of her tumultuous relationship with Jason over the past six years from beginning all the way up to the incidents that had occurred just the night before. By the time Amber was done, she was crying on Ms. Agnes' shoulder. She never realized how bad things were until she had actually heard herself talking about it.

"Amber, I can definitely help you get back on your feet, but you have to want this for yourself, not just for your daughter. Okay?"

"Trust me, I do." Amber glanced at the clock. "Ms. Agnes, I need to get to work, but I will call you later so we can work out the details."

After Amber left Ms. Agnes' home, she went in to work. Although Chloe and a few others noticed Amber's really quiet demeanor, no one mentioned anything to her. At six o'clock she left work, but instead of heading home she headed over to Danielle's house. Other than a few emails or texts, she hadn't spoken to her since the day she left her house to return back to Jason. Instead of using the key she still had, she rang the doorbell.

"Who is it?" she heard Danielle shout.

"Me, TT!" Ariel shouted

"Hey, baby girl." Danielle opened the door and picked Ariel up.

"Hey, D," Amber hugged her.

"Hey." Danielle hugged her best friend tightly.

"So, I've got some good news for you and I need a huge favor."

"Wassup?" Danielle asked while playing with Ariel.

"It's over, and I need you to keep Ariel for like a week while I get the situation handled."

"For good this time?" Danielle was a bit skeptical because they'd been down that road before.

"He did it in front of her," Amber admitted. "I never thought that would be a line he crossed."

"I'm sorry, Amber, I didn't really wanna be right. You know that?"

"Yea, I know."

"Ari, mommy's gonna see you this weekend, okay?"

"K, mommy." Ariel hugged her mother's neck tightly. "Love you."

"I love you, too, princess."

Amber left Danielle's house and on the way home, she picked up some boxes from the moving store. As usual, Jason wasn't home when she got there so she started packing and mentally preparing herself for the fight that was sure to ensue once Jason got home and saw what she was doing. Oddly enough, Jason never showed up that night. Amber loaded the boxes she had packed into her trunk and backseat before finally heading to bed.

Chapter 4

When Jason returned home the following morning, he started to notice that Amber's things were missing. He ran down the hall to Ariel's room and noticed the same there. He rushed downstairs to the kitchen and noticed a note on the table along with Amber's ring. The note read:

Dear Jason,

I love you more than words can express, but what we have and what we are going through is not love right now. More than that, I have to look out for Ariel. As her parents, it is our job to watch and protect her. I truly don't believe that what we have been through and are going through is not going to work because you don't want to take the time out to go and seek counseling.

I wish I could say that I saw a future for us, but as long as you refuse counseling, I have to refuse you and this relationship. I have no problem with you being a part of Ariel's life so long as you know those visit will have to be supervised. I hope we don't have to drag this thing out through the court systems, but if I have to then I will. Ariel is my number one priority right now and I will do everything in my power to make sure that she is healthy, happy, and protected.

I know that with the right help you will make an excellent father and husband one day. Jason, please for yourself, for me, and for your daughter, get some kind of help. I'm returning your ring because I don't think that you or I am ready for that type of commitment right now.

Love Always, Amber

Jason didn't know how to respond to her letter. Part of him understood where she was coming from, but the other half was seeing red, and that was the half that was ruling and reining him. He grabbed his helmet, got on his bike, and just rode until he could figure out what he was going to do to get Amber and Ariel back in his life.

Amber sat at the reception desk watching the children play over various security monitors stationed throughout Kids Corner Daycare. She zeroed in on Ariel's classroom. She never thought she'd see her three year old daughter so well adjusted after the turbulent start to life she'd had. Amber knew if she hadn't bumped into Ms. Agnes when she did, there was no way she and Ariel would be where they were today.

"Ms. Anderson?" Mrs. Daniels snapped her out of her daze.

"Huh? I'm sorry, what were you saying, Mrs. Daniels?"

Chloe Daniels was a five feet four, blond hair, blue eyed white girl who had the attitude of a sista from around the way. "What's going on with you today?" Chloe eyed Amber closely.

"I'm okay. I didn't sleep too well last night, but I'm good." Amber started shuffling through the files on her desk.

"Aiight then, are you and Ariel still coming over tonight for dinner? Thomas is grilling and inviting over a friend…"

"Chloe," Amber cut her off, "tell that husband of yours to stop trying to hook me up. I am so not trying to date anyone right now. Not in my condition."

"What do you mean 'not in my condition'?"

"Nothing, Chloe, nothing at all. We're still coming, but please tell Thomas I'm not interested."

"Okay, Amber, see you all at eight p.m." Chloe went back to her office.

The remainder of the day went fairly well. Amber was more than happy that it was Friday. Once all the kids were gone for the day, she and Ariel headed back to their room at Ms. Agnes' house. Amber and Ariel's room consisted of a queen size bed for Amber, and a small bunk bed in the corner for Ariel. There was a tall dresser that held both their clothes and bathroom. While this living situation wasn't what they were used to, it was a clean, quiet, and safe environment for the two of them. Amber felt like she had finally managed to undo all the damage that had been done in her life by Jason, and she was finally looking forward to a brighter future for herself, her daughter, and her unborn son.

When Amber arrived at Chloe and Thomas', house they were in the backyard with their five year old son, TJ, and Thomas' best friend, Kyle. Amber and Kyle had met a time or two before when he went to Kids Corner to do some construction work. Kyle was one of those guys that would easily get looked over because he didn't look like the money he made. He was a handsome six foot two, bald headed, evenly tanned white guy with the deepest blue-green eyes Amber had ever seen.

"Hey, Amber." Kyle walked over to her instantly.

"Hi, Kyle, how are you?" Amber shot Thomas and Chloe and evil eye.

"I'm great, how are you?" he asked as he handed her a drink. "Hi, little miss Ariel."

Ariel shied away from Kyle and hid behind her mother's legs. "Ariel, say hi." Amber gently pulled Ariel from behind her and held her hand to comfort her.

"Hi." Ariel waved at Kyle. "Can I go play with TJ?"

"Sure."

Ariel took off across the yard and joined TJ on the swing set. Amber thought she was the perfect blend of Jason and herself. Much like her father, she had a head full of naturally curly sandy-brownish hair, slightly slanted hazel brown eyes, and full lips. Like both of her parents, she was tall, especially for her age, and she possessed her mother's long, lean dancer figure and smooth cocoa brown skin.

"She's absolutely beautiful, but you already know that since she takes after her mother."

"Thanks." Amber blushed.

"So, can I be a bit forward with you?" Kyle shifted nervously.

"Umm, sure."

"I know you got a lot going on right now with Ariel and all, but I would really love to take you out on a date, get to know you better, allow you to get to know me better, and see what this friendship can blossom into."

"Kyle, I'm flattered, really I am, but I don't think that now is a good time for me to start dating someone else. I just got out of a really rough situation and I don't want to jump into something else until I am back on my own two feet."

"Amber, I'm not asking you to marry me, I just want one date, and if you don't wanna be bothered with me again after that, then fine."

"One date?" Amber debated in her mind if she should open the door.

"Just one date." Kyle flashed his irresistible smile.

"Okay." Amber took Kyle's phone and put her number in it. "Call me next week and we can arrange something."

"Great."

"Ay, Kyle, you think you could come help me over here on the grill?" Thomas called across the yard.

"I'm coming, man!" Kyle smiled at Amber once more then trotted across the yard to where Thomas was grilling.

While the men chatted and cooked food on the grill, Amber headed over to the swing set where the kids were playing and Chloe was sitting. As she walked over, she could see the nosy grin on Chloe's face and prepared herself for the pending interrogation. She took a seat next to her.

"I don't think it's a good idea to go on this date with him," Amber stated before Chloe said anything to her.

"Why?" Chloe could never really understand why Amber was so guarded.

"It's complicated," was all Amber said as she stared off into space.

§§§§§§

Keontay Vaughn is one of the newest up and coming authors in the Southeast. New York born, Atlanta raised, her love of the arts has pushed her to continue to hone her skills as a writer. In addition to novels, Keontay has a strong love of poetry and spoken word. Keontay released her debut novel *Behind Her Eyes* in the Spring of 2009. When asked why she writes she responds, "It's simple for me writing is like breathing, and if I ever stop breathing, my life is over, so my pen must stay in motion."

Ms. Agnes

After hearing several women come up and share their stories, and thank Ms. Agnes for helping them when they were at their absolute end, Talia approached the podium once more.

"Ms. Agnes, you are truly an angel on earth. Come on up and say a few words."

There was a thunderous applause. Ms. Agnes sat in her seat wiping her face with a handkerchief. When she woke up that morning, she had no idea the day would bring her such gifts. She loved how all her beautiful flowers had blossomed over the years. She looked around the room at all the smiling, strong faces. They were eons away from the frail, broken women she had first met. She knew then that everything she had done or tried to do over the years was worth it. She smoothed her dress, stood up, and slowly walked toward the podium. Once there, Story gave her a dozen long stem roses as Kyra placed a tiara on her head and kissed her cheek. Amber gave her a plaque of achievement for being so wonderful over the years and it had the names of all the women she had helped. She looked over at Mya, Jennifer, Tamika, and Talia and smiled.

She cleared her throat. "Well, I certainly didn't expect this when I woke up today." The room gave a slight chuckle. "I've been helping women for as long as I can remember. I think it was my calling in life, but it took a tragedy for me to realize that calling." Ms. Agnes teared up. "Over the years, I've always been asked one question that I've never answered for any of you ladies. Today, I think you all deserve that answer. I've locked this tragic incident away and hid it in the furthest depths of me, but it still makes me cry at night. Yes, I still cry. I cry for her every time I see one of your beautiful faces. I cry for her every time I see one of you butterflies blossom into your full being and are able to stand on your own two feet. I cry for her every time I lose one of you and you go back to your abuser. But today, I smile for her. I wear a proud smile for Abigail."

The ladies looked around at each other. The name Abigail didn't ring a bell to any of them. They focused back to Ms. Agnes to find out who she is.

"Abigail was my twin sister. You've all seen her. The picture in the living room with the girl about seven old playing in a field, looking happy and carefree, that's my Abigail." Everyone had seen the picture. They had assumed it was a picture of a young Ms. Agnes. "That was the only picture I kept of her because I always wanted to remember her being happy and carefree." Ms. Agnes sighed. "We were like two peas in a pod. You wouldn't see one without the other. That picture I have of her is rare. Our parents wanted to have a least one picture of us by ourselves, so they made us give each other ten feet of space, then snapped one picture, then the other. Soon as those pictures were taken, we were right back to each other's side." Ms. Agnes smiled at the memory of her sister, and everyone was even more interested in knowing what happened.

"Well, on our seventeenth birthday, we were at the county fair. Richard Moss had been sweet on Abigail for quite some time, but she was too wild and fancy free to let him court her. Richard had asked our parents if he could take Abigail out. They liked him. He was hard working and would be a great provider, so they allowed him to take her out on a date. You know how we girls are, we don't want to do anything our parents approve of, so she resented the date. To get back at them, Abigail made out with Richard on that first date. She was still a virgin, and the way he kissed and touched her made her feel things she hadn't felt before, so she had instantly become just as smitten with Richard as he was with her. They dated for a year and on our eighteenth birthday, Richard asked my parents for her hand in marriage. I hated him. Abigail spent all her time with him. Richard had stolen my best friend, so when I saw the bruises on her and I told daddy, he told me I was being silly and making things up. When I would ask Abigail what was going on, she told me I was jealous of Richard and trying to make everybody hate him so they would break up. I didn't want my sister mad at me, so I kept my mouth closed.

"Well, they got married, but I didn't see that same spark in my sister's eyes. I knew something was wrong, but she wouldn't tell me what. A couple of months later, she announced to the family she was expecting. I figured morning sickness had gotten the best of her and that was the cause of the rift I felt in her spirit. I kept a close eye out on her, but I couldn't keep a close enough eye because she was married and had moved out. She barely came around us anymore. I felt like a part of me was missing.

"One evening, I left to go see my sister. She was six months pregnant and I wanted to make sure her and the baby were doing OK. As I neared the house, I heard yelling. I tiptoed and looked through the window. I saw Richard push my sister so hard that she fell into the wall, and then he slapped her. I was livid, but I was scared. I wanted to run home and get daddy, but they had already thought I was making things up. I stood quietly in the bushes with tears flowing down my face as he called my sister a loose tramp and said the baby probably wasn't his. He pulled her up off the floor by her hair and pushed her roughly on the couch. He told her she better stay there until he came back and left out the house. When he jumped in the pickup truck, I ducked down, making sure he didn't see me. Once the back lights were far up the street, I ran in the house and held my sister.

"She was so frightened. I told her to get her things and come with me. She said she couldn't, he would come get her and hurt her more. She couldn't go back home to momma and daddy because she was a married woman and had to stay with her husband. She didn't have any place to go. I begged and pleaded with her to leave with me. Daddy would never let her be with a man that was hurting her. Abigail said that Richard loved her, but he just got the wrong impression since she made out with him that first night and thought she was a floozy. Richard was really the floozy. He had made out with all the girls, and rumor had it that another girl was pregnant at the same time my sister was."

Ms. Agnes was engulfed in emotions from that memory. She could still hear her sister cry. She could feel the fear Abigail had. She could see those bruises clear as day. Agnes knew why her sister hadn't been around. She had a black eye and a bruised lip. Patches of her beautiful black hair had been pulled out. There were bruises all over her arms. Agnes cried. If only she had made her sister leave that night. She knew if she had begged and pleaded just a few more minutes, she would have left. But, she didn't have a few more minutes. Richard had come back home. The both of them got scared and Abigail's eyes got as big as saucers.

"You have to leave, hurry," Abigail pleaded.

"Come with me."

"I can't. Just go. I'll leave tomorrow. I promise."

They heard the truck door open and shut, and Abigail begged with her eyes for Agnes to leave out the back door. Agnes hugged her sister one last time and left to run home and tell their daddy. As Richard walked in the front door, he heard the back door closing.

"Who the fuck you sneaking in my house?" He rushed to the back door and looked outside, but he saw nothing.

"What are you talking about? There was no one here."

"You think I'm stupid? You thought I was gone for the night, didn't you?"

"No, baby. I was just about to get ready for bed." Abigail got up and tried to nonchalantly walk past her husband. He wasn't going for it.

He grabbed her by her neck. "Who the fuck was that?"

"Baby, you're hurting me."

Richard squeezed harder. "You think you're going to make a fool of me? You think I'm going to sit up and take care of another man's baby?" Richard punched Abigail in the mouth.

Agnes gasped. She hadn't left just yet. She went back to her window to see what was going on. Seeing that, she ran around the house and went in through the back door with a brick.

"Get your hands off my sister!" she yelled in a shaky voice.

Richard laughed. He pushed Abigail to the side, making her fall and hit her head on the coffee table. Agnes ran to help her, but Richard grabbed her by her arm and threw her to the floor.

"You're just as pretty as your sister. You know, I flipped a coin to see which one of you I'd get sweet on. Abigail drew me in

because she didn't care if anybody was sweet on her. She's the kind that will be on that women's rights shit, marching and protesting. You are more of the marrying type." Richard sniffed Agnes and then kissed her neck. She squirmed and fought under him, trying to get away. "I bet you wouldn't give me all the trouble your hot ass sister has. She was always smiling at everyone, having all the guys want her." Richard undid his pants, then lifted up Agnes' skirt. "I bet you're still a virgin, huh?"

Agnes began to cry uncontrollably. She looked over at her sister and saw blood oozing from the back of her head. She hadn't moved a muscle since she went down. She was scared.

Richard pried her legs open and forced himself inside of her. He kissed her face as he roughly pumped in and out, seemingly turned on by Agnes' cries and whimpers. Finally, she just lay there and let him finish. Once he jerked and orgasmed inside of her, he grabbed her face roughly. "If you ever tell, I will kill your sister." He got up and kicked Agnes in her side, then left out the door.

Agnes crawled over to her sister, whimpering and coughing. "Abigail, get up."

She lightly shook her sister, but she wouldn't move. She finally looked over at Abigail's face. It was stone. Her eyes were still open and her face was wet from crying. Agnes let out a blood curdling howl. One of the neighbors heard and ran over to see what the commotion was about.

With the front door still open, Geraldine walked right in, asking Abigail what was going on when she saw the both of them on the floor. She saw blood and didn't know what was going on, so she rushed back to her house to call for help.

The pronounced Abigail and her unborn child dead on the spot. Agnes was rushed to the hospital because she was bleeding from the rape. She had a fractured rib that the doctors said would heal just fine, but she knew her heart never would.

She went into a shell after that, not speaking to anyone. She was angry with her parents for not believing her. She was angry with herself for not being there for her sister. Heartbroken, their parents sold the house and moved because they couldn't live in the *town where their daughter was murdered. Richard was sent to jail for life, but any memory of the town would bring them grief.*

They gave Agnes some money because she didn't want to move with them. She bought a small house a few towns over and found a job cleaning houses. The first woman she helped was someone she had seen on her route to work every morning. She would always look sad, and always had bruises. Agnes wanted to mind her business, but minding her business left her sister dead. She walked up to the lady one day and introduced herself, and told her if she needed, she had a place to go. That next morning, the woman had a small baby with her and asked if she meant what she said the day before. Agnes quickly took her back to her place and told her she was more than welcomed to stay for as long as she needed. She helped the woman get on her feet and saved up some money to send her back to the state her family was. That small gesture made Agnes so happy, that she did it again and again, and over the years, she has provided a place to go for those that thought they had nowhere.

"Ladies, I've never been in a relationship with a man that abused me, so I can't tell you know how it feels or how hard it may be to leave. All I can say is I'm proud of each and every one of you for taking that step on faith. I love you all, and as long as Ms. Agnes has breath in her lungs, you will always have a place to go."

DOMESTIC VIOLENCE FACTS

Domestic violence is the willful intimidation, physical assault, battery, sexual assault, and/or other abusive behavior perpetrated by an intimate partner against another. It is an epidemic affecting individuals in every community, regardless of age, economic status, race, religion, nationality or educational background. Violence against women is often accompanied by emotionally abusive and controlling behavior, and thus is part of a systematic pattern of dominance and control. Domestic violence results in physical injury, psychological trauma, and sometimes death. The consequences of domestic violence can cross generations and truly last a lifetime.

One in every four women will experience domestic violence in her lifetime.

An estimated 1.3 million women are victims of physical assault by an intimate partner each year

85% of domestic violence victims are women

Historically, females have been most often victimized by someone they knew

Females who are *20-24 years of age* are at the greatest risk of nonfatal intimate partner violence

Most cases of domestic violence are never reported to the police

Prevalence of Domestic Violence

- Estimates range from 960,000 incidents of violence against a current or former spouse, boyfriend, or girlfriend per year one to three million women who are physically abused by their husband or boyfriend per year.
- Around the world, at least one in every three women has been beaten, coerced into sex, or otherwise abused during her lifetime.
- Nearly one-third of American women (31 percent) report being physically or sexually abused by a husband or boyfriend at some point in their lives, according to a 1998 Commonwealth Fund survey.
- Nearly 25 percent of American women report being raped and/or physically assaulted by a current or former spouse, cohabiting partner, or date at some time in their lifetime, according to the National Violence Against Women Survey, conducted from November 1995 to May 1996.
- Thirty percent of Americans say they know a woman who has been physically abused by her husband or boyfriend in the past year.
- In the year 2001, more than half a million American women (588,490 women) were victims of nonfatal violence committed by an intimate partner.
- Intimate partner violence is primarily a crime against women. In 2001, women accounted for 85 percent of the victims of intimate partner violence (588,490 total) and men accounted for approximately 15 percent of the victims (103,220 total).
- While women are less likely than men to be victims of violent crimes overall, women are five to eight times more likely than men to be victimized by an intimate partner.
- In 2001, intimate partner violence made up 20 percent of violent crime against women. The same year, intimate partners committed three percent of all violent crime against men.
- As many as 324,000 women each year experience intimate partner violence during their pregnancy.
- Women of all races are about equally vulnerable to violence by

an intimate.

• Male violence against women does much more damage than female violence against men; women are much more likely to be injured than men.

• Women are seven to 14 times more likely than men to report suffering severe physical assaults from an intimate partner.

Domestic Homicides

• On average, more than three women are murdered by their husbands or boyfriends in this country every day.

• Women are much more likely than men to be killed by an intimate partner.

• Pregnant and recently pregnant women are more likely to be victims of homicide than to die of any other cause, and evidence exists that a significant proportion of all female homicide victims are killed by their intimate partners.

Health Issues

• The health-related costs of rape, physical assault, stalking, and homicide committed by intimate partners exceed $5.8 billion each year. Of that amount, nearly $4.1 billion are for direct medical and mental health care services, and nearly $1.8 billion are for the indirect costs of lost productivity or wages.

• About half of all female victims of intimate violence report an injury of some type, and about 20 percent of them seek medical assistance.

• Approximately one in five female high school students reports being physically and/or sexually abused by a dating partner.

• Eight percent of high school age girls said "yes" when asked if "a boyfriend or date has ever forced sex against your will."

• Forty percent of girls age 14 to 17 report knowing someone their age who has been hit or beaten by a boyfriend.

Domestic Violence and Children

• In a national survey of more than 6,000 American families, 50 percent of the men who frequently assaulted their wives also frequently abused their children.

• Slightly more than half of female victims of intimate violence live in households with children under age 12.

• Studies suggest that between 3.3 - 10 million children witness some form of domestic violence annually.

For more information or to get help, please call:

THE NATIONAL DOMESTIC VIOLENCE HOTLINE AT
1-800-799-7233
THE NATIONAL SEXUAL ASSAULT HOTLINE AT
1-800-656-4673
THE NATIONAL TEEN DATING ABUSE HOTLINE AT
1-866-331-9474

Lightning Source UK Ltd.
Milton Keynes UK
UKOW031919131212

203645UK00007B/322/P